"Once again Deborah Sprinkle has created a riveting page-turner in *Death of An Imposter.* Well-defined characters and a twisty plot kept me reading past midnight to find the killer."

— PATRICIA BRADLEY, AUTHOR OF THE LOGAN POINT SERIES, MEMPHIS COLD CASE NOVELS AND THE NATCHEZ TRACE PARK RANGER NOVELS

"Deborah Sprinkle has masterfully created a rollercoaster ride. Destination: to end a murder spree."

— DIANN MILLS, CHRISTY AWARD WINNER, LONG WALK HOME - JUNE 2019 TYNDALE, FATAL STRIKE - SEPTEMBER 2019 TYNDALE, WHERE TOMORROW LEADS - JUNE 2020 TYNDALE, AIRBORNE - SEPTEMBER 2020 TYNDALE, DIRECTOR: BLUE RIDGE MOUNTAIN CHRISTIAN WRITERS CONFERENCE

"Deborah Sprinkle has knocked it out of the park with **Death of An Imposter**! Her ability to draw me immediately into the story and keep me there, made this an almost impossible book to put down. She's an author that has catapulted onto my must-read list!"

— EDIE MELSON, AWARD-WINNING AUTHOR AND DIRECTOR OF THE BLUE RIDGE MOUNTAINS CHRISTIAN WRITERS CONFERENCE

DEATH
OF AN IMPOSTER

◆━━━━━━━━━◆

Deborah Sprinkle

FIRST PLACE
2018 Write to Publish
Thriller/Mystery/Suspense
Blue Seal Award

Scrivenings
PRESS
Quench your thirst for story.
www.ScriveningsPress.com

To Edie,
Thank you
so much for
your friendship
and your support! ♡

Deborah Sprinkle

Published by Scrivenings Press LLC
15 Lucky Lane
Morrilton, Arkansas 72110
https://ScriveningsPress.com

Printed in the United States of America

Paperback ISBN 978-1-64917-068-2
eBook ISBN 978-1-64917-069-9

Library of Congress Control Number: 2020948977

Cover by Linda Fulkerson, www.bookmarketinggraphics.com

All characters are fictional, and any resemblance to real people, either factional
or historical, is purely coincidental.

Scripture taken from the NEW AMERICAN STANDARD BIBLE®,
Copyright 1960, 1962, 1963, 1968, 1971, 1972, 1973, 1975,1977, 1995 by The
Lockman Foundation. Used by permission.

Published in association with Cyle Young of Hartline Literary Agency,
Pittsburgh, PA.

To Les, the perfect husband for me, and to God, who brought us together and continues to direct my steps for my good and His Glory.

ACKNOWLEDGMENTS

How do you thank an entire community of people adequately? I have no idea other than to say thank you fellow Christian writers. For your encouragement. For your support. For promoting my books ahead of your own. For showing the face of Christ to me and to the world. For teaching me by example how to be a better writer and a better person.

Specifically, I want to thank DiAnn Mills for her friendship, her amazing editing skills, and her counseling—not just for *Death of an Imposter* but for *Deadly Guardian* and other writings I have done.

Thanks to CW3 Larry Myers, US Army (Ret) who once again used his 30+ years of experience in criminal investigation in the Army CID, Tennessee Bureau of Investigation, and Criminal Investigation for the Department of Justice to help me with police procedure. I am proud to call him, and his wonderful wife, Nancy, friends.

Let me say here that I take full responsibility for any problems you may have with the actions of any of my characters. They sprang from my imagination and sometimes they proved to be a little hard to control.

And many thanks to my on-line Word Weavers group, Sandra M. Hart, Starr Ayers, Bonnie Beardsley, K. Denise Holmberg, and Linda Dindzans. All excellent writers themselves. You were the first ones to read *Death of an Imposter* and offer your praise and gentle critiques. I love you guys!

1

"If I weren't such a crusty old bird, I'd have my feelings hurt."
Aunt Rose handed her nephew, Dr. Daniel O'Leary, a platter
heaped with roast beef, sliced with surgical precision. "How long
will you be working at our little hospital?"

"Maybe a month." He forked a tender slab of beef onto his
plate. The real answer was as long as it took to complete his real
assignment. The one he couldn't share with his aunt.

He knew when he started working for the organization it
meant keeping secrets from Aunt Rose. Which hadn't been a
problem.

Until now.

He lived at one end of Ohio and she at the other. Misleading
his favorite relative on a long-distance phone call was easy. But
could he convince her of his lies face-to-face? More gray showed
in her auburn hair, and more lines radiated across her face, but
her gaze was as piercing as he remembered.

She chuckled. "I'm surprised your fancy hospital could do
without you for that long. Or are you really here on some secret
mission?"

Could she read minds as well? If so, he was doomed. "My
hospital in Cleveland is far from fancy, Aunt Rose. You know

that. We share staff now and again with other facilities. I'm only in Pleasant Valley as long as it takes to teach them the surgical procedure." He managed a wink. "Spending time with you is just a bonus."

"You always were a smooth one." She patted his hand. But was he smooth enough to get through the questions certain to be the evening's entertainment? Time for a diversion. "Tell me about Pleasant Valley. Do you like living here?"

"Sorry, Danny, my boy." She raised a brow. "But you'll not change the subject that easily." She poured more gravy over her meat. "What's this amazing new procedure you're here to teach our simple country doctors?" She waved her fork at him. "And don't say I wouldn't understand. I've been cutting up bodies since before you were born."

"I know that." Daniel smiled at her. "Why do you think I became a doctor?" Maybe telling her about the surgery would forestall other questions, and he could get away unscathed. Tonight at least.

He escaped her interrogation around eight and sat in his car for a moment before starting the engine. Did she suspect it was all a cover? He didn't think so. But he'd find out in the days ahead. At least he'd made it through the first trial, and it was good to see her.

Daniel navigated the unfamiliar streets of the small town and headed for the two-story house in the city the company had rented for him. He'd requested a garage, but did it have to be located in an alley?

Exhausted from all the mental sparring, he drove at a snail's pace along the narrow passageway between the garages. A scarcity of working streetlights, a new moon, and the cold drizzle that spattered his windshield left him squinting into the darkness. Eighth door on the right. Finally.

He jumped out, heaved the garage door up, and jogged back to the warmth of his car. Once he maneuvered his fire-engine red Infiniti into the small space, he shut off the engine.

Unease lifted the hairs on the back of his neck. Maybe he shouldn't have taken this assignment.

Too late now. He sighed and squeezed out of his car. Yanking the garage door down, he cringed at the squeal of metal against metal that cut through the still night. Whether the landlord paid for it or not, an automatic garage door and remote opener flew to the top of his to-do list.

Collar up and head down, he hastened across the meager back yard and took the four steps two at a time onto the covered porch, deep in shadow.

Hadn't he left the outside light on?

Footsteps sounded behind him. He whirled. A rock loomed above him. Daniel blocked the attack. But the blow sent waves of searing heat through his right arm and shoulder. He stumbled over a pot of flowers. Crashed to the porch floor. His head cracked against something hard. Pain shot through his skull with blinding whiteness. He fought to focus on his attacker.

Pale light from the kitchen window shone on the blurry figure standing over him, like a black and white TV screen with poor reception.

A fog of pain.

His attacker bent and peered at him. Daniel needed to act, but he couldn't move. Was he destined to die at the hands of a stranger? Adrenaline surged through him, and he fought the misery piercing his head. He shifted his body. Where was his gun?

The hooded figure straightened and disappeared into the nighttime gloom.

He fumbled for his phone and willed his shaking fingers to press the keys.

"911. What's your emergency?"

2

Throbbing forced Daniel's eyes open, and he moaned. Voices and a bright light. He attempted to raise his hand to shield his face and winced. His right shoulder and arm were shrouded in gauze.

"Lights down?" His voice was barely above a whisper.

A woman turned and approached his bed. "Good. You're awake, Doctor O'Leary." As she strode across the room, her black ponytail shone in the fluorescent lighting. "I'm Detective Bernadette Santos."

The scent of lemons and fresh cotton reached his nose. The overhead lights went off, leaving the soft glow of those directly over the bed.

"You're at Pleasant Valley Hospital. It appears you were attacked. Do you remember anything?"

Daniel peered at her through half-open eyelids. He needed time to think. Thoughts moved across his mind like a movie in slow motion. He'd only been in town a day. He shook his head. A wave of nausea hit him.

He swallowed. "I remember ... pulling into the garage."

"That's it?" She stared at him.

Memories from the evening flooded back, but he refused to

reveal more than he needed to say. Not until he had time to process.

"Yes." He closed his eyes.

"Do you know of anyone who might want to cause you harm?"

"No. Did the person break into my home?"

"Only if he or she locked the door when leaving."

Daniel kept his eyes shut. Did his attacker know the real reason he was in Pleasant Valley?

"If you think of anything, contact me. I'll leave my card on the bedside table." Detective Santos softened her tone. "I'll pray for your rapid recovery. Body ... and mind."

Startled, he stared into her deep brown eyes. She meant it.

"Thank you." The warmth of her voice lingered in his mind.

"One more thing." She turned a few feet away from his bed. "You can pick up your gun at the station when you get out." The door swung shut behind her.

His gun. He looked at the ceiling. He'd forgotten about that. Hopefully, the police hadn't searched the house and found his backup.

Gritting his teeth, he swung his legs over the side of the bed. A wave of dizziness caused him to grab the bedrail. He conducted a self-examination. A nasty bump on the back of his head. Possible concussion, but he'd take his chances. Tenderness in his left ankle when rotated. His right forearm was the worst. No cast, so not broken, but pretty banged up. And his shoulder hurt too. A little unsteady, but he had work to do.

Why hadn't he been killed? A warning?

He pushed the button to summon the nurse.

"Where do you think you're going, Mr. O'Leary?" She marched across the room to peer at his monitor and blocked him from standing, her body straining the seams of her uniform.

"It's Doctor O'Leary, and I'm checking myself out." He glared at her. "Either remove my IV or I will." He'd spotted gauze and tape by the sink. "And please bring me my clothes."

6

She stiffened. "I'll inform the doctor and be back to take care of your IV." She jerked her head toward a narrow door in the corner of the room. "Your clothes are in a bag in the closet. The EMTs cut the right sleeve of your shirt when they dressed your shoulder."

"Would you find me some scrubs, please? I'll return them."

He managed a smile. Who knows? He might be working with her in the future.

"Certainly, Doctor."

"Nurse, one more thing."

She turned, her purple nails drumming a staccato rhythm on the door.

"Doctors can be terrible patients, and I, for one, owe you an apology."

The woman regarded him with weary eyes. "Apology accepted."

In a few minutes, a younger nurse appeared with blue scrubs and removed his IV. "We're working on your paperwork, Doctor. It shouldn't be too long."

Fifteen minutes later, Daniel waited in a wheelchair for his cab, and another fifteen found him back at the townhouse.

He unlocked the front door, stepped to the alarm pad, and punched in the code. No one had entered his home. Including the police. Daniel breathed a sigh of relief.

The back bedroom had been configured into a small office. He slid his hand between the cushions on an overstuffed chair, and his fingers closed around the grip on his backup pistol. A Sig Sauer P238. He withdrew the gun, checked the magazine, and retraced his steps to the kitchen. His stomach growled, and he slapped a spoonful of peanut butter onto a piece of bread. Grabbing a diet soda, he sat at the small kitchenette by the window.

What *did* he remember? He drummed his fingers on the table.

A glint of red in the shadowy recesses of the hood? Maybe red hair?

Daniel flipped the porch's light switch a couple of times. Nothing happened. He stepped out, stuffing the gun into his waistband. A stepstool leaned nearby. He opened it and climbed the two steps. Dizziness assaulted him, but he needed answers. When he twisted the bulb in its socket, light shone on shards from the broken flowerpot scattered across the boards, dirt and trampled pieces of dead vegetation mixed in. His attacker had planned ahead. But why?

He combed through the debris for any possible clues. Nothing. Grabbing a broom, he swept everything into a black plastic bag and headed for the trashcans in the alley. The rain had stopped, but the air held the chill of early fall. The faint scent of logs burning in fireplaces triggered good memories from his childhood. Camping and hiking and—

A gate latch clicked across the passageway. Still on alert, Daniel closed the lid on his garbage can and slid into the inky black where his privacy fence met his garage. He was in no mood to socialize after the day he'd had.

A figure in an oversized hooded coat stepped through the gate, paused, and made the sign of the cross with a gloved right hand.

Daniel clenched his fists. His attacker stood less than twenty feet from him.

As if sensing another's presence, the hooded figure faced him. Daniel sprang from his hiding place and reached for his gun. The man bolted down the alley, arms and legs pumping. Ignoring the pain in his shoulder and ankle, Daniel ran after him.

Pools of light from the occasional streetlight spotlighted the man as he raced through the puddles. Shoes covered in muck, he slid and went down on one knee. A cry of pain.

Daniel surged forward, fighting against the ache in his leg. He couldn't afford a misstep.

The man regained his footing, and, with a glance over one shoulder, took off as if he were being chased by the devil himself. "Stop. I just want to talk." He couldn't do this much longer. His injured ankle and shoulder demanded attention like a crying baby. He found it hard to concentrate. His run became more of a limp hop, his ankle threatening to give out on him any second.

At the cross street, the figure sprinted to a white sedan. Daniel ran into the empty street. He aimed his gun as the car squealed away from the curb in his direction. Bright lights bore down on him.

"Stop."

The car's not going to stop. *Move.*

He stood frozen in place.

Brakes shrieked as the mid-size vehicle fish-tailed to a halt, the bumper inches from Daniel's knees. The engine clicked and sputtered in the quiet night, and Daniel stared at the obscure features within the hood.

Who was he, and what did he know? "Get out of the car. I just want to talk."

With another screech of tires, the sedan reversed, did a one-eighty, and disappeared around the corner. Daniel ran a few yards before collapsing on the curb.

Too dark to note the license plate number.

Could the hooded figure be the man he'd been sent here to find? He hoped not.

Or all those months of hard work were for nothing.

◁▬▬▬▬▬▬▬▬▬▬▬▷

HOODED FIGURES POPULATED HIS DREAMS, chasing him down dark tunnels and trying to run him over. Not the usual nighttime horrors, where he woke tangled in sheets and covered in sweat, but still. He yawned as he poured coffee into a travel mug. Aunt Rose expected him at her place of work this morning. He hit the house alarm button and headed for his car.

At a cross street, a white car passed in front of him. Right size and shape. Could that be the same car he saw last night? A glimpse of red hair in the driver's seat. He sped up and turned the corner. With no traffic, he slowed. Didn't want to spook the driver. Better to see where he went and confront him face to face. Daniel had a few questions for him. A stoplight ahead turned green. He needed a better look.

The white sedan turned right at the last second. Daniel gunned it. He rounded the corner and lifted his foot from the accelerator. The road stretched before him. Not a car in sight. Strip malls lined both sides of the street. He jerked his car into the first parking lot and rolled to a stop. White sedans riddled the area. He groaned and let his head drop to the steering wheel.

But then he saw a flash of red as someone emerged from a car at the far end. He drove closer, berating himself for buying such a distinctive car. He pulled down the aisle that gave him a view of the front of the white car. The person was standing next to it, fiddling with something. A woman. With magnificent fire-engine red hair. She glanced at him, turned, and rushed into a nearby store. Most likely to call the police about the man following her in the red Infiniti. Idiot.

◁·————————————·▷

SQUAWK. "LET ME OUT."

"Not yet, Lori Darling, I'm busy." Detective Bernadette Santos held a finger to her lips.

Squawk.

"*Amen.* One of these days, I'll learn to do my morning meditation in my bedroom." She sighed, laid her Bible aside, and opened the parrot's cage. Bernie pressed her hand against the shimmering green feathers of the bird's chest. "Step up."

The parrot jumped on her hand and climbed her arm to her shoulder. "Good morning, beautiful."

"Good morning to you too, Lori Darling." Bernie stroked the

bird's back. She liked having a pet again. Even if it was temporary. Parrots needed lots of interaction, and she wasn't home much. Eventually, she'd find a good home for Lori. One where the people could give her the attention she deserved.

Wonder if Daniel O'Leary was temporary? Bernie hadn't seen him around before last night, and there was something ... different about him. One of those guys who still manages to look good while lying in a hospital bed—a tangle of thick burnished copper hair above a square jaw and deep blue eyes—what she'd glimpsed of them. He barely looked at her. Was he in pain or hiding something?

"Since I've become a detective, I see hidden agendas everywhere." She laughed and shared the remainder of her toast with Lori before putting her back in her cage. "The poor guy had just been mugged and was in the hospital, and I've got him cast as a spy in town to steal Pleasant Valley's most valuable secrets. As if we have any." She tapped the cage. "See you later, sweet girl."

"Later, baby." Sunlight glistened off brilliant green feathers as Lori swung her head back and forth.

Ten minutes later, Bernie arrived at the police station. She pulled into a space with her name on it and clicked a picture of the sign. Her *familia* would be proud. It took her a year to make detective. Didn't seem that long ago since she sat in Madison Long's kitchen on guard duty with her detective manual in front of her.

She surveyed the building. A lot had changed in a year. Not only had she passed the exam, but the police department had moved to a bigger location where everything could be together on one floor, including the morgue. Pleasant Valley was growing, and they needed the space. She pushed through the doors to the precinct and slowed to a sedate walk. Her second day as a detective.

Was she up for the job? Many people believed in her, but did she believe in herself? She rubbed the medallion she kept in her pants pocket at all times. A present from Madison when she made detective, the shiny piece of silver held her favorite Bible verse. *Cease striving and know that I am God.*

Bernie peered over her partner's shoulder at the computer screen.

"Morning, Detective Santos." Detective Jeannie Jansen raised her head.

"Good morning, Detective Jansen." Bernie stepped back.

"Jeannie will do. We're partners now." She grabbed her phone and her purse. "And, we have a murder case. Let's roll."

A murder on her second day as a detective. She took a deep breath and touched her pocket. "I'm ready."

"You might as well drive." Jeannie tossed her the keys. "I need to tell you about the case."

"Yes, ma'am—I mean, Jeannie." That would take some getting used to.

Jeannie charged from the room toward the parking lot.

"I prefer Bernie, but—" She ran to catch up.

Jeannie stopped at a tan Dodge Charger, settled into the passenger seat, and opened the file. "Here's the address."

Bernie scanned the paper. "I know where it is." A section of town behind the library. Exquisite homes with large oak trees over a century old. She adjusted the mirrors and clicked her seatbelt. "What's happened?"

"Middle-aged man, Philip Majors, found dead this morning in his home. Someone called 911."

"That name sounds familiar." Bernie wove through the shaded streets of Pleasant Valley. Where had she heard it before?

Despite the beauty of each home, Philip Major's residence shone like a diamond among lesser gems. Bernie passed the mob of police cars parked haphazardly at the curb and continued to the end of the block.

"What are you doing?" Jeannie peered over her shoulder. "You missed our crime scene."

"I'm getting a feel for the neighborhood."

"Excuse me. I forgot you're one of those new 'whole-istic' policemen." Jeannie put her fingertips to her temples.

"Very funny." Bernie smiled and made a U-turn. In a way, Jeannie was right.

"Yeah, well, I'd like to see the body sometime this week." Bernie parked, but made no move to get out.

"Now what?"

"Nothing." She gazed across the immaculate lawn. Mr. Major did a beautiful job restoring the elegant two-story Georgian house. Yet, something about it ...

Bernie followed Jeannie to the door and nodded at her fellow officers along the way. Not long ago, she would have been outside keeping nosy neighbors away or stringing crime scene tape. If it wasn't for all the hard work it took, she'd pinch herself in amazement that this simple Latino girl from a poor family was now a detective on the Pleasant Valley Police Force.

They pulled disposable booties over their shoes and squirmed into nitrile gloves before entering the home.

"Wow." Jeannie's eyes widened. "I'd heard Major had redone the place, but I had no idea." She wrinkled her nose. "What's that smell? Sort of like rotten eggs."

"Reminds me of something." Bernie shook her head. "It'll come to me." She put her hands on her hips. Such beautiful woodwork and luxurious rugs. "Pretty grand. I wonder how he could afford all this on a dean's salary?"

"We'll need to check his financials. Good thinking."

Bernie stood a little straighter. "Where's the body?"

A nearby officer pointed toward the study.

Stepping inside, Bernie paused. Ahead two chairs faced a paneled wall with a fireplace. Floor-to-ceiling bookcases covered most of the other three walls.

"Who found him?" Bernie wandered to a drink cart and examined a sparkling cut-glass tumbler. Doubtful any fingerprints but Major's.

Jeannie consulted notes handed to her by the first officer on the scene. "The housekeeper. When she arrived this morning." She strolled the perimeter of the room.

A thick-set middle-aged woman appeared in the doorway.

"Ma'am, are you the housekeeper?" Jeannie approached her.

"Not for this grand house." The woman's piercing gaze swept the room before focusing once more on Jeannie. "I'm the new coroner." She shifted her case to her left hand and stuck out her right. "Name's Rose O'Leary. And who might you be?"

"Detective Jeannie Jansen." She grasped her hand. "This is Detective Bernadette Santos."

Bernie flashed her a smile. O'Leary? Could she be related to Doctor Daniel O'Leary?

"Jansen. I've heard about you." The corners of her lips turned up.

"What have you heard?" Jeannie snorted.

"Never get in a game of poker with Jansen—or something to that effect. Of course, I tend to draw my own conclusions about people," Rose said. "Now, where's my patient?"

Bernie had worked murder scenes before, but this one sent a chill up her spine. Dark oak-paneled walls swallowed the light from the fire and the few lamps in the room. Philip Major's body lay crumpled in front of the fireplace. A large blood pool under his head stained his exquisite Aubusson rug beyond repair. And that smell.

Rose maneuvered herself to her knees, her shadow shifting across the man's countenance. She flicked on her small flashlight.

"His skull's been crushed." She tilted her head toward a large rock a few feet away. "And there might be your murder weapon." She bent closer. "Someone didn't like the poor man. After the initial blow, there were several more."

Finishing her examination, Rose removed her gloves and packed her bag. "I'll do the autopsy as soon as I get back. Looks like he died where he fell. As for time of death, it's been about forty-eight hours. I'll try to get a more exact time but no guarantees." She touched her nose. "I guess you've noticed the lovely smell. I mean, the one not normally found around a dead body?"

They nodded.

"The rock used to kill him must have a high sulfur content." She shifted her bag and flexed her shoulders. "Others might call it brimstone—as in fire and brimstone."

Three pairs of eyes were drawn to the flames from the gas fire still crackling and sputtering before them.

Rose knelt by the hearth, her nose close to the floor.

"Where would you get a rock like that?" Jeannie said.

No response.

Jeannie glanced at Bernie and raised her eyebrows. "Doctor. I asked you a question."

"Help me up." Rose sat back on her heels and reached for Bernie's hand. Knees and back popping, she straightened. "I've changed my mind. I'm not sure the odor came from the rock. I believe the killer threw some sulfur into the flames before he or she left." She pointed to the fireplace. "Have your people check for residue. Of course, it could be both."

She fixed Jeannie with her gaze. "And the answer to your question is—I haven't the slightest idea." She grabbed her bag and headed for the door. "But I'll look into it. I'll let you know more after the autopsy."

"Can you put a rush on it, Doc?" Jeannie said.

"I make no promises. But I'll try." She paused in front of Bernie. "Oh, and I understand from my nephew that you're praying for him. God bless you. He can use all the prayers he can get. But what he really needs is a good woman in his life." She talked to the men picking up the body and left the house.

Bernie turned to see Jeannie staring at her. "Last night, at the hospital." She shrugged. "I told him I'd pray for him to feel better."

"Sounds like you may have put yourself in the running for Mrs. Doctor O'Leary." Jeannie grinned.

"Can we get back to work?" Bernie sighed.

"Yeah," Jeannie said. "Our victim was the head of—"

"St. Martin's Prep." That's where Bernie had heard the name. "Madison Long taught at his school."

"Who has he disagreed with? Fired? What kid has he kicked out, etc.?"

"What do you think the sulfur means?" Bernie suppressed a shudder.

"No clue." Jeannie clicked the remote, shutting off the gas fire.

Without the dancing flames, the room seemed even more foreboding. "I'll get forensics over here to check out the fireplace." Bernie slid her phone from her pocket.

After making additional notes and talking to the housekeeper, they left instructions with the officer guarding the property that no one be allowed on the scene unless cleared with Jeannie or Bernie. Outside, Bernie stopped in a patch of sunlight. The house may be beautiful, but the murder made it feel evil. A cloud passed over the sun, and she shivered involuntarily.

Jeannie's phone dinged with a text. "It's from Rose. She's done a preliminary examination of our body and wants us to get over there ASAP. She's found—"

"What?" Bernie frowned at her partner.

"The dead guy isn't who we thought he was."

3

"Let me drive. I want to get there this week." Jeannie held out her hand. "Besides, you may decide to get a feel for the neighborhood around the precinct."

"Very funny." Bernie tossed her the car keys and slid into the passenger's seat. "You do realize the man is dead? He's not going anywhere?"

"I know." Jeannie raced around to the driver's side "I just like to drive."

Back at the police station, Bernie pried her fingers from the handle above the door and got out. Jeannie was already inside. Bernie took several deep breathes as she raced to catch up.

They hurried down the corridor to a pair of double doors marked *Autopsy 101*. Through the window, Rose caught sight of them and held up five fingers. She consulted with someone whose back was to them, peeled off her gloves, and removed her lab coat.

"Let's go to my office." She smoothed her blouse over her sturdy figure and charged away, leaving the detectives behind. "I know my phone message was cryptic, but I'll explain." She stopped short. "Forgot my manners. Coffee? Soft drink? No? Okay."

Jeannie circled her finger at her temple.

"I saw that, young lady." Rose pushed through a door on the left.

Bernie bit her lip to keep from smiling.

"Sit." Rose shuffled through some files.

"We'd rather stand. Was the dead guy Philip Major or not?" Jeannie said.

"Yes and no. We knew him by that name, but ..." She pulled a piece of paper from a folder. "Ah. Here. His fingerprints. I ran them through the national database. Standard procedure. All educators are required to have background checks these days." Rose handed Jeannie the results. "As you can see, there was a teacher named Philip Major, but he died five years ago in Cleveland."

"Just about the time our guy came to town." Jeannie passed the paper to Bernie. "So, who is he?"

"I don't know." Rose shook her head. "Yet. I'm running his prints against all my databases. Since he assumed an identity, I'm guessing he's done something illegal, and his ID is in there somewhere."

What was he running from? Bernie tapped her finger on the report. This made things more complicated. Was he killed by someone he angered more recently or someone from his past who'd found him holed up in their little town?

"Thanks, Dr. O'Leary. Let us know when you find anything else," Jeannie said.

"Rose will do." She peered over reading glasses. "Don't you want to stay for the rest of the autopsy?"

Jeannie grimaced. "We have interviews to do at his school. Besides, I trust you."

"Hmm." Rose pushed to her feet. "Go on then. I'll see you at the poker game Friday."

"Yes, ma'am."

The door opened, and a tall man with deep blue eyes entered.

"Danny. I was hoping you'd make it back in time."

Rats. Bernie quickly scanned the room. The only exit was behind him. She arranged her petite frame and countenance to look like a professional and picked a piece of lint from her jacket sleeve.

"This is Detective Jeannie Jansen, and I believe you've already met Detective Santos." Rose gave her a sly grin. "This is my nephew, Dr. Daniel O'Leary. He'll be helping me here for a short while until his teaching position begins at the hospital."

"Nice to meet you." He extended his hand to Jeannie with a warm smile that went all the way to his eyes, then turned to Bernie. "Nice to see you again."

Did he just wink at her? She narrowed her eyes. "We need to be going. Let us know what you find on our John Doe."

Bernie avoided any contact as she squeezed past Daniel. He put a hand on the door, and she stilled.

"Since I'm new here, I'm eating by myself a lot. Would you consider joining me tonight?"

Slick. He asked in front of his aunt. She'd look like a heel if she said no. But she had a murder case. "I'm not sure—"

"We should be done by then," Jeannie said.

"In that case, I'd be glad to." Bernie clenched her jaw for a second and glanced at Rose. "Maybe your aunt would like to join us?" Two could play at this game.

"Sorry. I'll be working." Rose waved her hands. "But you go on. I don't eat dinner much anyway."

"If you're sure," Bernie said, "we could meet at Little Joe's Sandwich Shop at seven?"

"I was thinking more like Tony's Steak House. My treat. It will be nice to have someone across the table from me."

She forced a smile. Great. She'd have to wear a dress. She hated dresses.

"Suit up, my boy." Rose pulled on a lab coat and gloves. "How many autopsies have you done?"

"Not many." Daniel grabbed a gown from the pile. "But I'm sure I can manage." He studied his father's sister, his favorite aunt. A burning pain erupted in his stomach at the thought of all he was concealing from her. He popped two antacids into his mouth before pulling on his gloves. He had no choice, but that didn't make it any easier.

At least he really was a doctor and qualified to assist her. In fact, that's why he'd been chosen for this assignment and placed within the hospital while he investigated the suspect.

They strode into a room made of stainless steel and tile, but the powerful exhaust fans couldn't completely clear the sickening smell of death. Laminar hoods, cabinets, and sinks lined the walls. Three shiny tables stood in the middle. The one closest to them held a body draped in white. Rose led him to the corpse.

"The only thing I know is, our victim isn't who he said he was." Rose pulled the sheet back. "I'm running his prints through every database I have. I'm confident he's in there somewhere."

Daniel froze.

The man he came to find lay on his aunt's autopsy table.

"I need a minute." He rushed to the door, yanking his gown and gloves off as he walked.

Rose chuckled. "I wondered if you were ready for this."

In a quiet corner of the hall, Daniel pulled out his phone and punched in a private number. "I've found him."

"Great."

"But not the way we'd hoped. He's dead." Daniel thrust a hand through his hair. "He's been living under an assumed name. Do I tell them who he really is?"

"As long as you don't jeopardize your position."

He glanced down the hall. "Got it."

"Keep me updated."

He pressed *End*, took a deep breath, and returned to the autopsy room.

"You okay?" Rose glanced at him, her piercing gaze penetrating his soul.

"Yes." He took a retractor out of her hands. "You can stop your search. I know this man. He was a patient of mine in Cleveland."

She stared at him. "You're serious?"

"Afraid so. That's why I left the room." He shook his head. "It was a shock to see him lying there like this."

"We'll finish, and you can tell me about his real identity." She turned to the body lying before her and stuck out her hand. "Scalpel."

Daniel watched as his aunt made a perfect Y-incision. After five years in hiding, the company had received a tip to his whereabouts, sent Daniel to investigate—and someone bashed the guy's head in. Coincidence? Or was there somebody else looking for him too? Did the company have a mole?

"Grab that pan off the counter." His aunt held the man's liver supported in both hands. "And get me a new pair of gloves."

Daniel's attention snapped back to matters at hand. No time for speculation now.

After they cleaned up, the two sat across from each other in her office.

"Well?" she said.

He shrugged. "His name is Tariq Ghazzi. Originally from Turkey. An insurance agent if I remember correctly."

"That would make sense." Rose scribbled a note on her pad. "If he was Philip Major's agent, he'd have access to the documents used to change his identity. Anything else? What was he seeing you about?"

"Stress." Daniel kept his emotions intact. "He thought he was having a heart attack, but it was anxiety. I prescribed medication, and that seemed to take care of the symptoms." The pinch to his conscience was back.

"I'll need to call Jeannie." Rose picked up the phone. "She'll be glad to hear we have an identity."

And he'd have to alert his people to make sure his files reflected the story he just concocted. The police were sure to investigate.

"I wonder why he stole Major's identity. And why he came to Pleasant Valley of all places?"

Daniel sighed. He could tell her, but then ...

4

"Next stop St. Martin's Prep." Jeannie steered the car across town. "Maybe we should call Madison. She used to work here and could be a big help."

"She and Detective Zubari—"

"Captain Zubari, remember?" Jeannie signaled for a right turn.

Another change this year had brought. "She and *Captain* Zubari are on their honeymoon. I doubt they'd appreciate a call from us about a case right now."

"You don't think they'd want to help with a murder in their own backyard?" Jeannie looked perplexed.

Bernie shook her head. "Believe me, that's the last thing they want. I think we're on our own."

"I guess you're right." After a moment of silence, probably to mourn the passing of another of her great ideas, Jeannie cleared her throat. "We'll talk to each of the teachers and staff one on one. You take the women, and I'll take the men."

"Whatever you say." Bernie gazed out the side window. Why had she agreed to dinner with Daniel? She should have stood her ground, aunt or no aunt. Jeannie wouldn't do anything she didn't want to. She needed to be more like her.

"Of course, you're probably better with the men too. I'm not so good at the touchy-feely stuff." Jeannie frowned. "Maybe you should do the interviews, and I'll look at the records."

"That's fine." See? Even her partner thought she was soft.

They pulled into a visitor space in front of the school. "Ready?" Jeannie flung open her door, stood, and stretched.

Autumn filled the air. Clouds scudding across the blue sky made shadow movies on the grass. A cool breeze ruffled the leaves of the large oak trees shading the walkway.

"Did I ever tell you that schools make me nervous?" Jeannie said.

Bernie couldn't imagine anything making Jeannie nervous. Especially this stately red brick building. White double doors were centered under the pillared overhang. A man in dirty blue jeans and a T-shirt exited the building. Bernie registered the patch over his left knee with an STP sticker on it.

"Excuse me. We're looking for the office."

He jerked his head over his left shoulder. "There."

They scanned the large empty foyer before taking the door on the right where a slim woman hunched over a desk. Catching sight of the detectives, she corrected her posture and dabbed the tears from her eyes, revealing hot pink nails. Her nameplate read Ursula Pidgeon.

"May I help you?"

Jeannie and Bernie displayed their badges. "We're here to investigate the death of Philip Major. We need to speak with whoever is in charge."

"If you'll wait here, I'll inform Ms. Belkin, the acting dean." Ms. Pidgeon disappeared through a door behind her.

Jeannie strolled around the receptionist's desk and eased the top drawer open.

"What are you doing?" Bernie said. "We don't have a warrant."

"Hold your horses, Santos. It was ajar." Jeannie took a pen and moved some things around. "Just the usual stuff—pens, paper clips, note pads. Nearly empty hot pink nail polish. Wouldn't have expected that shade for our Ms. Pidgeon, would you?" The doorknob moved behind Jeannie, and so did she. She pushed the drawer to its original position and hurried to her former place.

Ms. Pidgeon reappeared and gave them a tight smile. "This way, please."

Bernie glanced at Jeannie, who looked like nothing had happened. Would that be her after a few years as a detective? Would she think nothing of bending the law occasionally? She hoped not. But for now, she had a job to do.

She took in the sumptuous surroundings. Thick carpet covered the floor of the spacious office. To the right, a loveseat and two chairs were arranged for easy conversation. A heavy oak desk dominated the far side of the room, positioned to take full advantage of the view of a private courtyard through two sets of French doors.

They approached the woman standing behind the desk. She was tall and broad-shouldered with short gray hair. Her handshake was firm, and her unpolished nails were bitten to the quick. No rings adorned her hands. In fact, she wore no jewelry at all. Ms. Belkin didn't fit with this elegant office, but judging from his home, Mr. Majors would have.

With jerky movements, she indicated two chairs in front of the desk.

"We're fine. Thank you," Jeannie said.

"This has been a terrible time for us here at St. Martin's." She folded her hands and placed them on the smooth oak surface.

The desktop was clear except for a lamp. No framed photos, pen, pencil, or notepaper. Not even a candy dish.

"We're sorry for your loss," Jeannie said.

"Thank you." She squeezed her hands together, her interlaced fingers blanching at the pressure. "I'm not sure what Philip's death has to do with the school since it happened at his home." She stiffened. "Surely you don't think anyone here was involved."

Philip? How close was she to the deceased?

"Simply routine. When we investigate a death, we talk to everyone who knew the victim. It helps us get an idea of what he was like." Jeannie smiled at her.

"May I ask how you heard about Dean Major's death?" Bernie said.

An unattractive flush spread from Ms. Belkin's neck to her cheeks. "One of our parents is highly placed in the police department. He felt it best I know about Philip—Dean Major's death immediately."

"I see." Bernie scanned the room. "Ms. Belkin, have you removed anything from this office? Photos? A pen set? A plant, maybe?"

"I'm not sure I like your tone, Detective." She rose. "Dean Major is—was—an extremely neat man. He always kept his office like this." She glanced at her watch. "If you'll excuse me, I have work to do. Ms. Pidgeon will assist you with anything else you may need."

"One more thing." Bernie stepped in front of her. "We need to talk to his staff and teachers."

"And examine his files," Jeannie said.

"His files? Why?" Ms. Belkin blanched. "Don't you need a warrant?"

"That's true, but Dean Major's files could contain something that would help in our investigation, and we assumed you'd be as anxious as we are to find who did this as quickly as possible." Jeannie closed her notebook. "But if you insist on a warrant ..."

"No. Do what you have to do. The problem is ... we can't seem to find Dean Major's files."

"They weren't on his computer?"

"I already told you. This was his office. No computer." She gestured around her. "He was old school and kept paper files. We searched everywhere, but we have no idea where he kept them.

Maybe you'll have better luck than we did. In the meantime, I'll have Ms. Pidgeon bring Dean Major's staff in for interviews. You can tell her in what order you'd like to see them."

"Before you go, maybe you could tell us where you were two nights ago," Bernie said. "That way, we won't have to bother you again."

Her jaw clenched. "I was at a conference in Chicago for private school administrators. I just got back yesterday. I'll have Ms. Pidgeon text you the information." She spun on her heal and stomped off.

Bernie eyed Jeannie. "This is getting more complicated by the minute."

"Do we know anything about his family?" Jeannie examined the sturdy desk. "Maybe there's a secret compartment somewhere." She tapped on the paneling. "Or, in the wall."

Bernie consulted notes on her phone. "No known family."

"Wonder if Rose had any luck with his fingerprints?"

"I haven't heard anything yet." A credenza against one wall held a small refrigerator with soft drinks and water. She could use a bottle of water about now. "He's got to have a computer out there somewhere." Bernie surveyed the room again. "We'll have it mirrored. Chances are his dealings are hidden there. Our techs need to see it."

Jeannie stretched, an audible cracking coming from her back. "I guess we'll be doing interviews together. Let's start with the head of the English department, Henry Abbott."

THEY CHOSE the seating area to conduct their interviews. Each detective took a chair, while their interviewee sat on the sofa.

"Detectives, I may as well tell you right now I didn't like Philip Major, and I can't say I'm sorry he's dead," Mr. Abbott said.

Bernie studied the man on the sofa. Immaculately groomed,

calm, hands folded in his lap, dark eyes focused on Jeannie. A glance between the women. Jeannie would take this one.

"What was it about Mr. Majors that you didn't like?" Jeannie said.

"He was an odious man." Abbott scratched his nose. "He took every opportunity to kick people when they were down."

"Give me an example. How did he hurt you, for instance?"

"I was one of the candidates in the running for his job. He found out and spread vicious rumors that I was an alcoholic. Needless to say, I couldn't prove where they came from, and I was barely able to keep my job as an English teacher." He smirked. "Ironically, afterward, rumors spread that he sold drugs."

"Was he? Selling drugs?"

Abbott shrugged. "Who knows. All I know is, he must have crossed one person too many. Or crossed the wrong person."

"Where were you Friday evening between nine and midnight?"

"Am I a suspect?"

"At this point, everyone who knew him is a suspect." Jeannie waited, pen poised above her notepad.

"I was at home alone."

"Do you have anyone who could corroborate your story?"

He shook his head. "Wait. I may have called my co-worker. I can't remember."

"Your co-worker's name and phone number?"

"Wendy Green. If you give me something to write on, I'll provide all her information."

Jeannie tore a piece of paper from her book and slid it across the coffee table to Abbott.

"Anything else you can tell me?"

"I know he fired people for ridiculous reasons. One of my friends was fired for cooking burgers in her homeroom class. She should have been reprimanded, certainly, but not fired. My guess is she made too much money, and Major needed to balance the budget. That's the kind of man he was."

"Sounds like you and others had reason to dislike him." Jeannie closed her notebook. "Don't leave town, Mr. Abbott. We may need to talk with you later. Here's my card in case you think of anything that could help." She rose. "One more thing. Do most of the teachers feel the same way?"

"Yes, Detective. I'd say we all do."

◁▭▭▭▭▭▭▭▭▷

BERNIE'S TURN. She considered the woman perched on the couch. Slim. Medium height. Light blue eyes behind heavy framed glasses. Brown hair. Something odd there. A wig. Maybe thinning hair? Chemo?

"I'm so sorry for your loss, Ms. Pidgeon. How long did you work for Dean Major?"

"Thank you." She blinked away tears. "I've been his assistant since he came to St. Martin's Prep."

"That's a long time." Bernie looked at her notes. "Did you like working for Dean Major?"

She sighed. "He could be difficult at times, but I've worked for far worse. He was very particular, that's for sure. No margin for error with him." She clenched her hands in her lap.

"I understand." Bernie jotted a note into her phone. "Did he have any friends or colleagues that he hung out with?"

"Excuse me." Ms. Pidgeon snorted and raised a hand to her mouth. "I never saw or heard him speak of anyone. He was a very private person."

"What about enemies?"

"He could be very abrasive at times." She crossed her arms over her stomach. "And he wasn't very diplomatic when it came to handling the teachers or staff. I'm sure many of them were upset with him—" She leaned forward and caught Bernie's attention. "But not enough to kill him. Detective, I'm sure no one at St. Martin's did this horrible thing."

"Has anything strange happened within the last few days or weeks?"

She frowned as though searching for something—anything that would lead them away from her beloved school. "No. I can't think of a thing."

"I have to ask," Bernie said. "Where were you Friday evening between nine and midnight?"

"Me?" The woman swiped a trembling hand across her forehead. "Let me see. Friday. Was that the day I went to the movies with ...? No." Her lower lip quivered. "I guess I have no alibi. I was at home. Alone." She slumped back on the cushions of the couch.

"Thank you, Ms. Pidgeon. We may need to speak with you again later—"

"Hang on." The woman sat up and raised a slim finger. "I did think of something strange. About a week ago, a woman came to register her child for the next semester. She was sitting at my desk, filling out paperwork, when I heard Mr. Major's door open behind me. She looked up, turned pale as a ghost, and left mumbling something about feeling ill." She paused. "I turned to find Mr. Major staring after her."

"What happened then?" Bernie gripped her phone. Could that be the break they needed?

"I asked if he was all right, and he snapped at me. Then slammed the door." She shrugged.

"Do you still have the form she was filling out?" Bernie said.

She shook her head. "Sorry. I threw it away."

"Do you remember her name or anything about her? What she looked like?"

Ms. Pidgeon's eyes widened, and she moved forward on her seat. "She had red hair. A beautiful color. I remember commenting on it. And sparkling green eyes."

"Good." Bernie nodded encouragingly. "What about her name? Anything?"

"I only remember thinking it didn't go with her looks—you know, she looked Irish, but her name wasn't Gaelic."

Bernie made a final note. "You've been a big help. If you remember anything else, please call." Bernie handed her a card.

"Detective Santos," Ms. Pidgeon said. "I heard there was the smell of sulfur in the room where he was killed." Fear rose in her eyes. "You won't find Dean Major's killer among the living. He sold his soul to the devil long ago, and Satan came to collect." She crossed herself before slipping through the door.

5

B ack at their police-issued Dodge, Jeannie handed the keys to Bernie and climbed into the passenger seat. "I'm so tired, I don't know if I can eat." Jeannie leaned back on the headrest and closed her eyes.

"Does that mean we skip lunch and take a nap?" Bernie started the car. She wouldn't mind.

"No. We'll take turns. This time, I'll nap, you drive." She smiled—her eyes still closed.

"I'll hold you to that, partner." Bernie accelerated into traffic. "Where to?"

"Fried chicken. I feel like something greasy."

"I'm not saying a word." Bernie cringed. Was it too soon in the partnership to be kidding with Jeannie like that? But she'd fallen asleep. Good. She needed it. This was going to be a tough case. Nobody liked the victim. Ms. Pidgeon claimed he'd been murdered by the devil. Wonder where she heard about the sulfur smell? Bernie believed in evil. But the evil she'd seen was flesh and blood.

The car stopped, and Jeannie woke with a start. "Where are we?"

"Lunch. Fried chicken just like you ordered."

Inside a popular restaurant, they chose a booth that afforded them the best view of the entrances and counter out of habit. Shortly thereafter, their chicken orders arrived.

Jeannie finished chewing and gulped diet cola. "According to the teachers, Majors ranked right up there with Attila the Hun. Only one woman said anything nice about him. She liked the way he dressed." She belched. "Excuse me."

"Same with the staff." Bernie wiped ketchup from her mouth. "Ms. Pidgeon seems convinced he sold his soul to Lucifer, and he decided it was time for Major to pay up."

"Never heard that one before." Jeannie barked a laugh. "But considering what we're learning about this guy, it's beginning to sound like a plausible theory." She licked her fingers and wadded her napkin. "You finished? We need to get back at it."

"Somebody evil did this. They're alive and breathing, and it sounds like we have plenty of suspects." Bernie nudged a hand into her pocket and grasped her medallion. *Lord, be with us.*

"Yeah. And I have a feeling there are more to come."

Bernie shivered as she left the restaurant. A change from sunshine to gray skies and a biting wind reflected her unsettled mood. This morning, she relished the challenge of a murder case in her first week as a detective. They'd visit the scene, follow the clues to the killer, and make an arrest. Not that she expected it to be that simple, but the reality of Philip Major's life and death threatened to be far more complicated than she'd hoped for.

As an officer, she'd seen death in all its forms, but she'd never been the one tasked with discovering the who, when, and why. Now her first case, and the corpse turned out to be an imposter, a bully, and everyone in his life seemed to be a suspect. Where should they begin?

"You drive. I've got a message from Rose." Jeannie clicked her buckle. "Whoa. It seems her nephew, Daniel, recognized our John Doe. He was a patient of his in Cleveland. An insurance salesman."

"Great. What's his name?"

"Tariq Ghazzi." Jeannie jotted it down in her notebook. "Originally from Turkey." She chewed the end of her pencil. "I would have said he was Italian. He reminded me of my uncle."

Back at the station, seated once more at their desks, the women searched the internet in an attempt to find something about their victim. Nothing. No Tariq Ghazzi in Cleveland appeared in any database.

Frustrated, Bernie closed her computer. "We know who our dead man is, but what good does it do us? Do you think he's in witness protection?"

"Could be." Jeannie stretched. "Rose is still working on his fingerprints, but if he's under wraps, she won't find a thing." She glanced at the clock. "I know a guy who may be able to help us. But he's in D.C. I'll wait until morning to call."

"I need to go home." Bernie shuffled papers on her desk.

"Oh yeah. You've got a dinner date with the doctor," Jeannie said. "Have fun."

Bernie scowled. "Right. See you tomorrow."

"While you're whispering sweet nothings in each other's ears, find out if he knows anything more about our victim."

"There will be no whispering, but I will definitely try to get more information about our victim."

◁▭▭▭▭▭▭▭▭▭▭▷

LOCATED SNUGGLY between a vanilla two-story and a gray story and a half, Bernie's deep blue single-story house with black shutters served as an anchor in her life. She needed a house like this. A sanctuary. She had family, two sisters and a brother, but they were grown and moved away. Her mother was dead, and her father—he might as well have died the same day as her mother.

Bernie slammed her car door. Enough. She had a date tonight with a man she barely knew and needed to psyche herself up for it. Didn't help that she felt this crazy attraction to him. Maybe a shower would help. Hot water beat her muscles into submission.

35

A faint sound. Bernie shut the water off. Was that the doorbell?

"Get the door." Lori screeched from her cage in the living room.

It sounded again. She grabbed a towel and pulled on some sweats. Peeking through the spyhole, she saw her father leaning against the wall outside her house. She threw open the door. "Papá, what are you doing here?"

"Can't a father visit his daughter?" Victor Santos tripped and caught himself on the doorframe.

Bernie grabbed his elbow. The smell of cheap wine hit her, and she wrinkled her nose.

Wolf whistle. "Hello, handsome."

He straightened. "You have company?"

"It's only my parrot." Bernie guided him to a chair.

"Sit over here by me, good looking."

"Lori Darling, stop." Bernie wagged a finger at the bird.

"It's been a long time since I have been called that." Her father laughed. "Where did you get such a fine bird?"

"I rescued her from a crime scene." She sighed. "Her owner passed away, and no one wanted her." Bernie planted her fists on her hips. "Papá, you're drunk."

"Maybe a little." He held up two fingers about an inch apart.

She glared at him.

"Don't look at me that way." His face crumbled. "I miss your mamá so much. She was my life." He placed his hand over his heart.

"I know." Bernie blinked back the tears that sprang to her eyes every time she thought of her mother. "I miss her too." She bent over her father, trying not to inhale too deeply. "Let's get you settled in the guest room. You'll sleep here tonight."

She helped Papá into the bedroom and onto the bed. He grabbed her arms. "You find the devils who killed your mother, Bernadette. Promise me."

How could she promise him? It was so long ago. And yet, he was her father. How could she not?

"I promise." She pulled the covers up to his chin. "Now rest. I have a date tonight. I'll be back later."

"A date? With a nice Hispanic boy?" His heavy eyelids lifted a fraction.

"*Sí.* Now go to sleep." Another lie. Bernie gently closed the door and went to her bedroom. The last thing she felt like doing was going to a restaurant with a man she'd just met.

She surveyed her image in the full-length mirror. Long-sleeve dark green dress and black pumps, with a sweater in case the restaurant was chilly. Her shoulder-length dark brown/black hair, brushed to gleaming, pulled into a ponytail, and small gold hoop earrings. Should she use more make-up? A little lip gloss, perhaps.

And a purse big enough to carry her gun. She smiled. Most women worried about their phone or lipstick. She preferred to have her pistol on her person, but she never got used to a thigh holster under her skirt. That's why she hated wearing a dress. No place to put your firearm.

Before leaving, Bernie checked on her father. Grief and alcohol had aged him beyond his years. Pain stabbed her chest. She'd request her mother's file tomorrow. For now—she looked at the table beside the bed—she'd take her father's car keys to protect him the only way she knew. After covering Lori's cage to keep her quiet, Bernie was out the door.

All the way to the restaurant, her twenty-six-year-old mind grappled with what her twelve-year-old eyes saw all those years ago when Mamá was shot. Witnessing her mother's brutal murder motivated her to become a policewoman. But until now, as a detective, she hadn't the means to investigate her case. Would she be able to bring her mother justice after all these years?

She pulled into the restaurant's parking lot and spied Daniel emerging from his red car. A loud crack sounded—a sound

Bernie knew too well. She slammed her car into park, wrestled her gun from her purse, and rolled out her door onto the pavement. Taking cover between two parked cars, she cautiously raised her head to scan the area.

Daniel lay motionless on the asphalt next to his car. Her heart lurched.

A young man in a valet's uniform ran from car to car, clearly intent on reaching Daniel to help him.

"Go back." She popped up long enough to draw his attention and ducked down again. "I'm police. The shooter may still be out there. Stay put. I'm headed your way." Sirens wailed in the distance.

She bolted around her car and paused. No shots. She dashed to where the valet huddled behind a sedan. "I hear sirens. Has someone called 911?"

He nodded.

"Good. You wait here for them. I'll go see about the man who's been shot." She gave him a tense smile. "What's your name?"

"Patrick." A tremor in his voice.

"You're doing great, Patrick." The sirens were getting closer. Staying low, she moved to where she could see Daniel, lying in a small pool of blood. "Daniel? Can you hear me?" She crawled to him and placed two fingers on his neck. A pulse.

He groaned and stirred.

"Don't move. Looks like you've been shot." Bernie laid a hand on his back. "Help is on the way." Hoping the shooter was long gone, she knelt and observed Daniel's car more closely. The bullet had shattered the window behind the driver's seat. She frowned. How could a bullet break that window and hit Daniel getting out of the car? She crouched, careful not to touch anything, then turned in a slow arc, probing the shadows for unusual shapes.

An ambulance and two police cars bumped into the parking lot, red and blue lights flashing.

Across the street, a hooded figure stared in her direction.

"Police." She raced toward him. When she hit the street, he sprinted away into the darkness. "Wait."

Cars rushed at her, forcing her attention on her own game of red light, green light so that by the time she arrived on the other side, he was nowhere to be seen. She raked a hand through her hair, unraveling her ponytail. A light-colored pickup pulled into traffic a quarter-mile away, tail lights winking in the night.

By the time she crossed back to the restaurant, police had cordoned off the area around Daniel's car, and EMTs knelt by his side.

"I'm a cop." Bernie laid her gun on the ground and held her hands in the air. "Don't shoot." After showing them her credentials, Bernie returned to Daniel, who was sitting on the ground, propped against his vehicle.

<hr />

"You'll have one awful headache, Dr. O'Leary, but that beats being shot." The EMT gathered his trash and closed his case. He helped Daniel to his feet. "Head wounds tend to bleed a lot, as you know, but it looks worse than it is. Keep an eye out for concussion. You know the signs."

"Thanks." Daniel rubbed the back of his neck. Hope the guys back in Cleveland never heard about this one. When his window exploded, he dove for the ground, hitting his head on the edge of his car door on the way down. Knocked himself clean out. He surveyed his bloody clothes. No steak dinner tonight. Worst of all, Bernie saw the whole thing.

"How're you feeling?" She gave him a gentle smile.

"Embarrassed." He dropped his gaze to her dress, streaked with dirt. "I'll pay for your clothes."

She glanced down in surprise. "No need. I'm just glad you're okay. You almost got killed." She stared at him. "Why would someone do this, Daniel?"

"Probably just a random drive-by." Dangerous ground.

"Not in this neighborhood." Bernie scrunched her brow. "You seemed to be the target. The question is, why?" She rubbed her arm. "You want to grab some sandwiches and eat them at my place?"

He liked Bernie—a lot—but if he planned on seeing this woman, he'd have to be on his toes. She was smart. Worse, she knew how to read people. And he was no match for her tonight.

"I think I'd better take a rain check." He placed his hand on her arm. "But thanks. Another time."

She stepped back, her eyes darkening. "Sure. Another time." She smiled, and the warmth returned to her eyes. "You've been through quite a bit in the last couple of days. Get some rest. I'll see you tomorrow."

His stomach clenched as he watched her walk away. She knew he was hiding something, and she didn't like it. What had he gotten himself into this time?

WHAT WAS DANIEL HIDING? Bernie recognized one of the policemen on the scene. "Freddie, did you figure out where the shot came from?"

"Looks like the shooter was on the second floor above the deli." He pointed to a building across the street. "Must have been a pro. No prints. No brass. Nothing." He sighed. "Only way we could tell was from the angle of the bullet. It lodged in the doc's dashboard."

"Keep me in the loop. Okay?"

"Sure. Congrats on making D."

"Thanks."

He eyed her dress. "You just happen to be here?"

"Something like that."

⟨⊶━━━━━━━━━━━━━━━━━━━⊷⟩

BERNIE CREPT down the hall to her bedroom. Her father slept peacefully, and Lori must be asleep as well—at least she was quiet. She glanced in the mirror. Another one bites the dust. That's why she hated dresses. She'd take it to the cleaners and see what they could do, but she didn't hold out much hope.

After another shower, she slathered peanut butter on a piece of bread and smoothed grape jelly on another. Slapping them together, she cut the sandwich on the diagonal the way her mother did. Some potato chips rounded out her meal, and she grabbed a diet iced tea before carrying her dinner into her room.

Daniel O'Leary had lied to her. Maybe not with what he said —more like with what he didn't tell her. He knew that shot was meant for him, and he probably knew why. There was more to him than those deep blue eyes and great smile. She'd known it the first time they met.

And she'd find out.

Her first week as a detective, and she already had two mysteries to solve—one official and one personal. But equally intriguing. Could they be linked?

She studied what they'd gathered about the Philip Major/Tariq Ghazzi case, reading through every interview and making notes. When she exhausted the day's information, her thoughts turned to Dr. Daniel O'Leary. She pulled his gun from her purse—SIG Sauer P226. Only his fingerprints on the grip, and his license checked out.

On a whim, she searched online for Daniel's background. Bachelor's degree in biology at Kent State. Received his M.D. from Case Western Reserve in Cleveland. Specialty in orthopedic surgery. Worked at various hospitals in Cleveland. Why was he here? Something about a teaching job? How could all this have anything to do with who shot at him tonight? Or the attack the night before? Only a rookie cop believed in coincidences.

She entered his rental address, and a Zillow listing popped up. Same neighborhood as Philip Major. She pulled up a map of the area. An alley separated their backyards. Daniel was Philip's (Tariq's) neighbor. She crossed her arms over her chest as her mind raced with the possibilities. One man killed and another targeted. Living in houses back to back. Were they involved in something in Cleveland that followed them to her small town? Criminals?

Or could the unthinkable be true? Daniel killed Tariq. Her mouth went dry.

But who would be gunning for him?

7

"Thanks, Officer." Daniel dragged up the steps to his front door. His head pounded, and all he wanted was to go to bed.

A note lay on his welcome mat. He grabbed it by a corner and stepped inside. Through blinding pain, he eased onto the sofa and opened it.

That was a warning. You did what you came to do. Now go back to your own people and leave us alone.

"You did what you came to do," he whispered. What did they think he did? And who were his own people?

Placing the note in a plastic bag, he deliberated his next step. Sending it overnight to Cleveland would take a while to get results, and he was doubtful the techs could pull prints from the paper. He could show it to Bernie. But she wouldn't be satisfied with investigating the origin of the note. She'd want to know everything. And he couldn't do that. At least not yet.

He'd sleep on it and call his boss in the morning.

If he lived that long.

BERNIE JOLTED AWAKE, spilling her notes and computer to the floor. Samba music filled her small home. Who was in her house? She grabbed her gun. Back against the wall, she moved down the hall. Bathroom. Clear, but towels on the floor. She lowered her gun. Spare bedroom. Clear. Ruffled bed. Of course. Papá. She slipped her gun into the back of her pants. Now she remembered. She rubbed her eyes and rounded the corner into the kitchen.

"Good morning, beautiful." Squawk.

"Good morning, *mija*." Her father navigated around her kitchen, her parrot on his shoulder.

"Same to you guys." Bernie chuckled and pulled a chair out at the small table.

"I made you breakfast." He removed two perfect eggs from the skillet and placed them on a plate. Setting two cups of coffee on the table, he took the chair across from her.

"I want you to stay here today, Papá." She sipped her coffee. "We can talk about the future when I get home. Okay?"

He returned to the sink. "Sure, my daughter. Anything you say."

<hr />

VISITING Daniel O'Leary at home was not a good idea, but something nagged at her. Besides, she might learn something. And she could return his gun.

Bernie nodded as she considered the row house before her. Much more inviting than Philip Major's classic French style home with its elegant mansard roof. The cemetery across the street held grand old trees and elegant monuments. A peaceful view. Glancing at her watch, she climbed the steps and rang the bell.

"Detective Santos." Daniel held the door open. "Come in."

"I thought I'd see how you're doing this morning." Boxes

stacked in the rooms to her left and right. "Did you sleep well? No headache?"

"I'm fine. Thank you. Do the police in Pleasant Valley usually make wellness calls on victims?"

"No, but I was in the neighborhood." She pulled his gun from her purse. "And, I thought I'd return this while I'm here. You forgot to pick it up yesterday."

"Thanks. After seeing Tariq on that autopsy table, I guess it slipped my mind." He placed it on a nearby table and gestured down a short hallway. "Would you like some coffee?"

"Any tea? I've had my quota of coffee for the morning."

She followed him down the hall. Someone had done a good job planning the cozy kitchen. Small, but efficient. Although, the pale green walls, light cabinets, and marble countertops were too bland for her taste.

"I can do tea." He opened a drawer and frowned. "Once I find it."

"Mind telling me why you were carrying?"

He put a mug of water in the microwave and pressed some buttons. "Habit. When you travel around Cleveland all hours of the night like I do, it's good to have a firearm."

She sat at a little table by the window. "The shooter last night was professional, by the way." She paused. "Not a drive-by. Why would a hitman be after you? Does that have something to do with Cleveland too?"

"I can't imagine what." He shrugged with his back to her. "Mistaken identity? What else can it be?"

"Tariq Ghazzi lived across the alley from you."

"Are you interrogating me, Detective?" He dipped the teabag in the hot water.

"Always. It's in my blood. It's just ..." She looked out the back window. "So many things. You're attacked. The same night Ghazzi was killed. The victim lived by you. You knew him from Cleveland. And then you get shot at." She shook her head. "Upsets my sense of equilibrium."

"I can see how it would. But this is a small town. And despite what they teach you in cop school, coincidences do occur." He set the tea in front of her.

"Maybe." She wrapped her hands around the warm mug. "Thanks." The morning light shining through his window highlighted the sprinkling of freckles across his nose and cheeks. A lock of his russet hair curled in the middle of his forehead, and she had an urge to brush it into place. She blinked and took a sip. Steady girl. "I need to be going."

"You haven't finished your tea." He laid a hand on the table between them.

His look sent a tingle down her spine. The last time she'd been alone with him, he'd been in a hospital bed.

"I hate to be late on my third day on the job."

"Just made detective?"

"Yes."

Admiration shone in his eyes. "Congratulations. That's a real accomplishment. And closing a murder case is a great way to start your career."

"As long as I—we can solve it." She placed her hand against her pocket.

"You will. I'll walk you to the door."

She stood and tugged at the hem of her jacket. "What did you do after you got home from the hospital the other night?"

"I was wiped out." He avoided her eyes as he opened the door. "I had a little something to eat and went to bed."

"Too bad." What was he hiding? "You'd make a great witness." She held out her hand to shake.

"I'd like to try for dinner again soon." He took her hand in his.

Warmth traveled up her arm to her cheeks. "I'll check my calendar and—"

Daniel yanked her toward him. They fell back onto the floor in a clumsy embrace. The air exploded with the staccato sound of bullets ripping through brick, wood, and glass. Tiny piercing arrows of shrapnel rained down on them as they hugged, each trying to protect the other.

An eerie silence followed.

"I think they've gone." Bernie pushed against Daniel. What seemed so natural a second ago, took on an awkwardness that made her blush. She rolled away from him and sat. Grabbing her phone, she called dispatch. "Shots fired at 188 Virginia. We need backup, forensics, and medical." As she spoke, she studied Daniel for any signs of injury. "Are you hurt?"

He scooted over to sit against a wall. "Nothing serious." Wincing, he moved to his feet, retrieved his gun, and checked the magazine.

A little too natural in her opinion—like he'd done it many times before.

"No bullets?" His mouth twisted into a grimace. "You gave it back without my bullets?"

"Yes. I did." She glared at him. "That's department protocol."

He headed to the kitchen and returned, slamming a magazine into the pistol while he walked. "They may come back to finish the job before backup gets here."

A chill went through her. Who was he? She pulled her firearm from its holster.

Daniel moved to the windows at the front of the house, edged one side of the curtain, and peered out. "Call your guys back and tell them to pull into the alley. I think the sniper's in the graveyard across the street."

"Why?" She moved toward him. How did he know this stuff?

"Just do it." He waved her back. "Please."

Who did he think he was ordering her around? But then, better safe than sorry.

"Dispatch, tell all personnel to come through the alley." However, she wasn't alerting the force to a sniper without probable cause. "You'll have to give me a reason to call out the big guns."

"Come here."

She moved behind Daniel and peered out the window.

"Watch the crypt with the praying angel on top. Can you see the occasional glint of reflection around the left side?"

And there it was. "You think it's a scope?"

"I do."

She dialed dispatch for the third time. "Possible sniper in the graveyard across the street. Will need SWAT." Daniel O'Leary had some explaining to do.

A call came through.

"What's going on out there?" Jeannie's voice carried through the phone.

"I stopped by to return Doctor—"

"I'm waiting to go over the case with you, and next I hear, you've got the SWAT team called out for a sniper."

"There's been a shooting—"

"I'm on my way. You can tell me then."

Bernie sighed. Her short career as a detective flashed before her eyes.

"Hey." Daniel touched her arm to get her attention. "Don't worry. You did everything right."

"How would you know?" Frustration burst from her. "You're only a doctor. Supposedly."

He gave her a quirky smile. "I watch a lot of *Law and Order?*"

She eyed him. Definitely too cute for his own good. And funny. A laugh bubbled up inside her. She pressed her lips together.

"When this is all over, you and I are going to have a heart-to-heart about the real Daniel O'Leary."

His smile faded. "You know why I'm here, and you know my aunt. If that's not enough ..." He stared at the cemetery. "Run a background on me."

"I already have. For all the good it did me." Somehow, she didn't feel like laughing any longer.

Sirens sounded in the alley. Soon, EMTs and police flooded the house. Detective Jeannie Jansen among them.

Akin to a human hurricane, she burst onto the scene and whisked Bernie off to a secluded corner. "What happened?"

"This morning—"

"And I want details. The whole story."

"Okay." Bernie formed her thoughts. "I stopped by Daniel— Doctor O'Leary's to return his gun and check on him." She continued from there as Jeannie took notes, interrupting to clarify a few points. Bernie studied her. "So, am I okay?"

"What are you talking about?" Jeannie grimaced.

"I'm not in trouble?"

"You mean just because you called out SWAT on your third day on the job?" Jeannie's eyes twinkled. "No, but be ready for some ribbing." She closed her notebook. "What do you make of this guy Daniel?"

Bernie shook her head.

"I get the feeling he's mixed up in our other case somehow— beyond knowing the guy." Jeannie turned to where Daniel talked to an officer.

"He knows more than he's saying. And I'm not sure his background is correct," Bernie said.

"Me, either." Jeannie pulled on her earlobe. "He seems interested in you. We could use this to our advantage."

Bernie's heart rate increased. "What do you mean exactly?"

"Nothing bad." Jeannie waved her hand. "But another dinner or two. Movie, maybe. Get to know him. That sort of thing."

That she could do. In fact, she wanted to see him again. She'd show him he couldn't charm her into ignoring what was right in front of her own eyes.

But did he want to see her after learning she'd been checking up on him?

8

B ernie redid her ponytail with practiced movements and approached Daniel. "Have you given your statement yet?"

Daniel nodded. "What did SWAT find?"

"I don't know yet." She hesitated. "Does the offer for dinner still stand?"

"Well, that depends." He knew in his gut it was a bad idea, but ... "Are you going to interrogate me?"

"Not at dinner." She flashed him a smile.

"Then, sure. When? Or do you still need to consult your calendar?"

"Is tonight too soon?"

He kneaded the back of his neck. "I'm still pretty shaky. Is tomorrow night okay?"

"Same place, or does that have too many bad memories?"

"I don't let things get to me. Same place. Same time."

"See you then." As she turned to go, her arm brushed his.

A spark of electricity shot through his body.

He watched her drive away. No way he could tell her any of the truth and expect her to help. She'd want the whole story, and his bosses would object. Too bad. She was the first woman since —in a long time—he felt he could trust.

Maybe even learn to care for.

Closing his eyes, he relived the scene from two nights before. He should have taken the shot, but instead, he froze. Was he ready for this? Maybe he'd returned to active duty too soon.

After a deep breath followed by a few painful flexing exercises, Daniel took his coffee onto the back porch. He felt bad about withholding evidence that could help solve a murder. But how could he get the white car and a description of the hooded figure to the police without looking like that's just what he'd done? Maybe an anonymous tip?

His phone rang. Unavailable number. The boss. "Yes?"

"You have a new assignment. You are to find out who killed Tariq Ghazzi. Maintain your cover."

"I understand, but somebody thinks I assassinated Ghazzi and wants me gone. It would be a lot easier if I could bring local law enforcement into my confidence."

"Sorry. Not an option at this time."

He frowned. "What about sending me help from there?"

"We can't afford the manhours for this assignment. Besides, it would only call attention to you and break your cover.

"I've already been shot at twice and had a threatening note left at my house. You don't call that attention?" He pinched the bridge of his nose.

"We'll give you a contact you can use for information to complete your new assignment."

"Is that the best you can do? Fine." He tossed the phone on the table and stared into space. Another job to do. And he would do it.

Or die trying.

Tires screeched on the street. Daniel grabbed his gun. He flattened against the wall where his silhouette wouldn't stand out against the evening sky. Now, to wait.

"Danny, my boy. Where are you?" Rose O'Leary rushed around the corner of the house.

Aunt Rose, God bless her.

She stopped short. "Put that thing away, Daniel O'Leary." She waved at the gun he held behind his back. "You could hurt someone. Namely, your dear old aunt."

"Sorry. I'm a little jumpy about now."

"That's why I'm here, dear boy." She followed him into the house and inspected the living room, murmuring prayers as she picked her way through the debris littering the floor. "I'll help you clean up this mess." She returned to the kitchen. "But first, let's have some tea."

He steeled himself for his aunt's questions. In fact, he had a few of his own for her. He came to find Ghazzi, which he did. Now Daniel's boss wanted him to find Ghazzi's killer without breaking cover. She was his entry into the case, and he intended to make good use of the only legitimate connection he had. Aunt Rose would be his unwitting accomplice, feeding him the information he needed to get the job done.

He hoped.

"Boy, how long have you left that bag in the water? It looks like coffee, not tea."

"Sorry. I'll make you another." He poured the ruined beverage down the sink.

"I'll do it." She grabbed the mug. "Sit. Rest your weary mind."

"How did you hear about the shooting?"

"It was all over the scanner. I could hardly finish my work." Her eyes filled with concern. "If my assistant hadn't been out sick, I would have legged it."

"What did you hear? I mean, did you hear anything about a sniper?" A headache formed between his eyes.

"Yes, and my blood ran cold as the Irish Sea." She paused. "Why do you ask?"

"I'm the one who spotted the flash. Now I'm wondering if I was mistaken." He smiled at her. "Would you ask Bernie if they found any evidence of a gunman in the graveyard for me? So I don't feel like a fool?"

"I can do that." She took a sip of tea. "Daniel, what's going on? Mugged, shot at twice, and a past connection to a murdered man."

He put his head in his hands. "I honestly don't know. I wish I did." Deception sliced through his heart, and he ached to tell her the truth.

"Why don't you stay with me for a while?"

"I wouldn't do that to you." He shook his head. "If someone is after me, I'd be putting you at risk too." He rose and walked to the window. "Besides, they said a police car would be stationed outside for a couple of days. I'll be fine."

"At least let me help you clean up." Rose stood, knees cracking.

"Thanks, but the police said to leave it for now."

"I'll let you rest." She joined him and patted his arm. "You know I love you, sweet boy."

"I love you too, Aunt Rose." He swallowed a lump in his throat.

Once she'd left, he paced the back porch. Should he ignore orders and confide in his aunt? She might feel obligated to tell the police or want to investigate. More importantly, she could become a target as well.

And what about Bernie? He trusted her. But she went by the book and was new on the job. He plunked down onto a metal lawn chair. She'd already been in the line of fire once because of him.

No. He couldn't risk breaking cover. The shadows lengthened in his backyard until they melded together into inky blackness. He rose and stretched. Tonight, he would sleep. But tomorrow ...

Tomorrow he would start fishing for a killer.

And he'd be the bait.

BERNIE PULLED INTO HER DRIVEWAY. Her father's car was gone. She dumped her purse on the seat beside her. His keys tumbled out along with her wallet, lipstick, and all the other necessities she carried. Yep. She still had them. So how could his car be missing? She rubbed her forehead and crammed everything back into her bag.

As she opened her front door, a rush of air and flapping wings came at her from the right. She threw her arm up in response. Lori Darling landed on a chair next to her.

"What are you doing out of your cage?" Bernie nudged the bird on her feathered chest. "Step up." She carried her parrot back to the cage and scanned the room for damage. "Looks like you were a good girl today."

"Good girl." Lori swung her vibrant green head back and forth.

"But, where is Papá?" Bernie pulled her phone from her pocket. It rang four times before going to voicemail. "Papá, I thought we had a deal. You were supposed to stay with me again tonight. Where are you?" She pressed *End* and stared at the phone. She'd managed to get the file on her mother's killing, and she'd hoped to go over it with him tonight. Maybe he would call her back before he had too much to drink.

Please, Father, look after my papá. I couldn't bear to lose him too.

9

The hair on Daniel's arms raised the minute he stepped into the police station. He stopped a passing officer. "What's going on?"

"They found a possible witness in the Major killing. He just got here."

"Great." He headed for the morgue. A witness? Was someone else in the alley that night?

Rose sat at her desk, reading glasses perched on her nose. "Danny, my boy. Sure you're ready to come back?"

"I was dying of boredom at home." He dropped into the chair across from her. "I hear they're questioning a witness?"

"A bum." She nodded—her attention focused on the paper before her. "Saw a man run into the street from the alley and get into a car. Another man ran out and tried to stop him." Rose peered at him. "Are you sure you're okay? You're pale."

Should he stay and discover what the guy saw? Or should he leave and wait for the police to show up at his door? "I'm fine. What's on the agenda for today?"

◦———————————◦

BERNIE HADN'T SLEPT WELL. She kept expecting the doorbell to ring. The hot shower helped, as did three cups of black coffee.

What was she thinking? Bernie threw dirty towels into the washer and pushed start. She had no time to take on her mother's fourteen-year-old case right now. She had a murder case of her own and a man with a secret she determined to discover.

"Bye, Lori. Be good."

"Later, baby." Squawk.

BERNIE ENTERED the precinct and glimpsed Daniel headed toward the morgue. Her stomach fluttered. She'd catch up with him later. Right now, she had a witness to question.

Someone sprayed air freshener in the small interrogation room, but the scent of lilacs was no match for weeks of body odor and unwashed clothes. She smiled to mask the grimace that was her natural response.

"Good morning, sir. Are you comfortable? Have everything you want?" She took a seat and opened her file.

The man gave her a toothless grin and scratched his head of oily salt-and-pepper hair.

"Good." Where was Jeannie?

The door opened and slammed against the wall. "Let's get started." Jeannie yanked the chair out next to Bernie and dropped down. After going through the introductions for the recorder, she gave Bernie a thumbs up.

"Art, tell us what you saw the night of October sixth. Take your time."

"I was sleepin' in the doorway of the Chinese restaurant on Howard Street when this guy comes tearin' out of the alley—"

"What did he look like?" Jeannie looked up from her notes.

"He had on this hoody thing."

"What did it look like?" Bernie said. "Was it long? Short? Black? Gray?"

Art scratched his chest. "Kind of long, and I think it was gray."

The same guy across from Tony's Steak House when Daniel was shot at?

"Did you see his face?" Jeannie said.

He snorted. "No way. It was too dark."

"Then how do you know it was a man?" Bernie said.

Art frowned. "Gosh. I never thought of that. Guess it coulda been a woman. He—she—it was kinda small."

"Go on," Bernie said.

"Can I just say he?" His eyes darted between the two women.

"Sure." Bernie smiled at him.

"He ran across the street to a car." He looked at Jeannie. "A white car. I don't know what kind. Then another guy comes running out of the alley and into the middle of the street." He leaned forward. "The car screeches away from the curb, headed straight for the second guy. 'Bout gave me a heart attack." His hand flew to his chest. "The guy in the street just stood there with his gun pointed right at the—"

"Whoa. Where'd the gun come from?" Jeannie stopped writing.

Art shook his head. "I don't know. One minute he's standing there, and the next, he's got a gun in his hand."

Jeannie twirled her finger in the air, indicating that Art should continue.

"Anyway, the driver hit the brakes and came within a hair of hitting the guy in the street." Art sighed. "They just sat there. Looking at each other for a long time. Then the car backed up and sped away."

"What did the second guy do?"

"He kind of stumbled over and sat on the curb for a long time. Then he got up and went back down the alley."

"Would you recognize him?"

"Oh yeah. I got a good look at him." Art's brow scrunched.

"You're not going to believe this, but I think I saw a guy here who looks a lot like him."

The two detectives shared a knowing glance.

"Let's go for a little walk, Art." Jeannie took his arm.

◁———————————▷

DANIEL, fully gowned, gloved, and masked, handed his aunt the Stryker saw and watched intently as she made the cut. The patient was an elderly woman who died from a fall. Straightforward, but an autopsy was required because it happened in a long-term care facility.

He caught the faces out of the corner of his eye. Jeannie, Bernie, and a man he didn't recognize appeared in the window of Autopsy Two. The witness? He squeezed the forceps in his right hand. Would they be waiting for him when he was done?

"Daniel, pay attention. I need a pan for the brain."

"Sorry."

His aunt placed the pan on the scale. "One thousand, one hundred, ninety-six grams." She set it aside. "I can finish here. Why don't you go on home and rest? You've been through a lot."

"I am pretty tired." He came around the table. "I'm supposed to have dinner with Bernie tonight, but I'll have to see how I feel."

"Willing to try it again, is she?" Rose snorted. "Brave lass." She waved over her shoulder. "I'll check on you later."

He cracked the door from his aunt's office and peered into the hallway. Jeannie, Bernie, and the man stood at one end, heads together in conversation. Now was his opportunity. He slid through the opening and started toward the exit. A glance over his shoulder told him they were turning his way. Opening the door to his right, he stepped inside. A broom closet. He pressed his ear to the door. Couldn't hear a thing.

The dial on his watch glowed, and he decided to give it twenty minutes. He flipped a bucket upside down and sat, leaning his head against the wall. He must have dozed off because when he looked at his wrist, half an hour had passed. This was ridiculous. He opened the door a crack and listened. Nothing. Wider. No one in sight. A spot between his shoulder blades itched all the way to his car, urging him to move faster. It was all he could do not to run.

10

B ernie left the stationhouse and checked her phone again. No calls. Maybe her father's car would be at her house. She sped up. Normally the sight of the two-bedroom bungalow caused her breathing to slow and the tension to ease in her body. But today, the deep blue siding and black shutters didn't calm her soul.

His car wasn't there.

Why did it matter? Sometimes months passed without hearing from him. Why was she so uneasy now? Because he'd never brought up her mother's case before. He'd never begged her to find out who killed her, and she'd never promised before.

Was he talking about it at the bars? Maybe the wrong people heard his rantings and were afraid he'd go to the police—try to get the case reopened. A chill went through her.

Lord, protect him.

She took a deep breath and willed her mind back to the matter at hand. Dinner with Daniel.

"Hello, beautiful."

"Hi, sweet bird." Bernie threw her keys on the counter and headed for the bedroom. "No time to chat right now."

"Lori needs a snack." The brilliant green bird flapped her wings.

Bernie laughed. "Of course, you do." She grabbed some peanuts and crossed the room to the birdcage. "I'm sorry."

Ten minutes later, Bernie stepped from the shower and dressed for her dinner date. This time, she wore black dress pants and a silky jade-colored top. No more dresses. Her hair lay in a loose braid over her left shoulder, and her best gold hoop earrings adorned her lobes. She looked good, and she knew it.

BERNIE SPIED him standing on the sidewalk outside as she exited her car. She paused a moment to savor the aromas of grilled steak, onions, and garlic drifting through the air.

"Wow." Daniel opened the door to Tony's Steak House for her. "You clean up good, Detective."

"Thanks. You don't look so bad yourself." His deep blue button-down collar shirt matched his eyes perfectly, and the rich fabric of his tie made her want to reach out and touch it. She let the corners of her lips lift in a soft smile.

"What?"

"Just thinking it's nice to have a relaxing evening out."

They took some time to decide on their food order, discussing the pros and cons of different cuts of steak and what salad dressings each preferred. After the waiter left, Daniel placed his elbows on the table and leaned toward Bernie.

"What was that all about today with you, Jeannie, and that guy touring the precinct?"

She folded her hands in her lap. "He's a witness who might be able to help us with the Philip Major case."

"Really? How?"

"I guess it doesn't matter if I tell you. You'll probably hear about it anyway." She studied the open and honest looking face of the man next to her. Why was she hesitating?

"He saw the perp run out of the alley and another man chasing him. The odd thing was, the witness thought he saw the second man entering the stationhouse when he got there. We took him around the building to have an informal look at all the men, but he couldn't ID any of them. Jeannie's with him right now going through all the precinct's photo IDs."

Daniel's stomach rolled. He reached for her hand. "Can I ask you a personal question?"

"That depends." She eased her hand away.

"I've noticed you touch your right leg when you're nervous. Were you injured?"

"When it seems I'm touching my leg, I'm really tapping my pocket." Bernie reached into her pants pocket and withdrew her medallion. She pushed it across the table toward Daniel. "This is why."

He looked askance at her before picking up the token. "Psalm forty-six, verse ten." He turned it over. "It's beautiful."

"Madison Long Zubari gave it to me when I made detective." Bernie folded her hands on the table. "I was one of the officers assigned to her case. Her now-husband, Nate, was the investigating detective along with Jeannie. That's how Madison and Detect—Captain Zubari met."

"I've heard the story." Daniel placed the silver piece of metal in her hand. "Several people ended up murdered, and someone tried to kill her and Captain Zubari as well, right?"

"Yes. She became a close friend." The brush of his fingertips sent sparks up her arm. "I keep it with me always."

"I can see why."

Their food arrived, and conversation slowed.

Bernie's phone buzzed, and she pulled it from her purse on her lap. Jeannie had an ID on the second man. She froze. The noise of the restaurant receded into the background. *Dear God, no.* She sipped her water to ease the pain in her chest.

"Doctor O'Leary, we need to take a ride to the station." She couldn't look at him. He'd lied to her. Sat there and asked her about the witness knowing all along. Her throat constricted, and she couldn't speak.

He placed his napkin on the table and called for the check.

Once outside, she turned to him. "Can I trust you to meet me there?"

"Bernie, I—"

"Please, don't say anything." When she gained the privacy of her car, she banged the steering wheel with her fists. What a fool she'd been. She was beginning to like him. She called Jeannie. "We're on our way in."

"Sorry to ruin your night, kid."

"Just doing my job."

DANIEL PULLED into his parking spot at the station. Taking this assignment had been a mistake. He covered his face with his hands. The pain in her eyes haunted him and would for a long time. He wanted to tell her the truth. But would she believe him? Or would she believe he'd killed Tariq Ghazzi?

And what about the people targeting him? Who were they? Would they go after Aunt Rose and Bernie?

He couldn't let that happen.

11

Bernie stood in the hall, heart pounding. She'd rather take a bullet than go into that interview room, but she bowed to her partner's years of experience.

"You've spent more time around him and can read him better than I can," Jeannie said. "I'll conduct the interview, and you watch him for signs of inconsistencies. Jump in any time you feel you need to." She shuffled her files around in her arms. "Come on, Santos, it's just another interview."

Tell that to her rolling stomach.

The harsh light in the room bleached Daniel's skin and accentuated his freckles, but his eyes remained the deepest blue she'd ever seen.

Jeannie arranged the chairs so that Daniel sat with his back close to the wall. She positioned her chair directly in front of him, their knees about a foot apart. An open file lay on a table to her right. Bernie sat farther back on Jeannie's left. This was their standard set up. They could see the body language of their interviewee, and by moving her chair closer, Jeannie could apply subtle pressure without using words. It worked—most of the time.

"Doctor O'Leary. We have a witness who swears he saw you

chasing a hooded man out of an alley the night Mr. Majors—Tariq Ghazzi—was murdered." Jeannie consulted the file next to her. "What do you have to say about that?"

"He's right. It was me." He propped his right leg on his left and gazed at the detectives. "I went into the alley to put out the trash, and there he was, coming out of the yard across the alley."

"So, you just decided to go after him? Not knowing if he had a gun or a knife?"

"I know it was crazy, but at the time, all I thought about was catching a bad guy."

"A macho man thing?"

"Look." He placed both feet on the floor and leaned forward. "It was stupid. I realized that after it was over. That's why I didn't say anything to the police."

Jeannie held a photo of Tariq Ghazzi in front of him. "And when you found out the dead man lived across the alley? Didn't you put two and two together? Why didn't you come forward?"

Daniel rubbed his forehead. "By then, I didn't think you'd believe me. Especially since I knew him in Cleveland. I was afraid I'd look like a suspect."

"You're asking me to believe—" Jeannie held up three fingers "—number one, you assumed the man leaving someone else's backyard was also your attacker." She bent one finger. "Two, you had no idea Tariq Ghazzi lived across the alley from you." Two fingers bent. "And three, a smart guy like you thought telling lies and withholding information was a better idea than coming clean to the cops." Jeannie scooted closer. "Trust me. I'm not buying it."

"I understand your reservations."

"I don't think you do, Doctor O'Leary. What did you plan to do if you caught the guy?"

"I wanted to stop him, see that he was arrested, and press charges."

"What about the gun?" Bernie said in a low voice. She'd taken his gun from him in the hospital. How did the witness see him with a gun pointed at the car?

Daniel stared at her. He held his hand in front of him and folded all his fingers back except his pointer finger and his thumb. "He must have seen me do this."

Possibly. It was dark, and the witness had been awakened from a drunken stupor. She'd let it go for now.

"Did you recognize the perp?" Jeannie said.

He shook his head.

"How about a description of the car?"

"A white sedan. That's all I could see in the dark."

Jeannie jotted a note in her file. "Doctor, how do you explain the attempts on your life?"

He pinched the bridge of his nose. "I can't. I wish I could."

"Was there any other involvement between you and Mr. Ghazzi in Cleveland?" Bernie made a note on her phone.

"None. I promise you. He was my patient for a brief time. That's it."

"Okay." Jeannie aligned the papers in her file. "We could charge you with obstructing justice, doctor. But your aunt is the coroner, so we'll give you a pass—this time." She tapped the table next to her. "If you see or hear anything else in your neighborhood again, you better be on that phone to us pronto. You understand?"

"Yes, Detective."

Bernie pushed her chair back and left the room. At the vending machine, she slid her card and pressed the buttons for the largest chocolate bar available. He'd outright lied about the gun, and as for the rest of the interview, he managed to keep from telling the whole truth. She gritted her teeth.

"I know I'm the last person you want to see right now, but please, Bernie. I could go for an ice cream sundae right now. How about you? Daniel's sad reflection caught her gaze in the glass front of the candy dispenser.

"No, thanks. This will be fine." She retrieved her chocolate bar and turned to march away, but instead, spun on her heel and stomped back to him. "Why?"

He took a step backward. "Why what?"

"Why do you want to go have ice cream with me after being in that interrogation room?"

He placed a hand over his heart. "I like you. And, I'd like to get you know you better."

"I value honesty in a relationship, Daniel, whether it's a friendship or something more."

"I get it." He sighed. "Please. It's just ice cream."

She studied him for a moment. "Let me get my purse."

"Great. What's open this time of night?"

"I'll meet you at Little Joe's Sandwich Shop."

They drove separately and parked around back.

"You're determined to eat here. I should have agreed the first time." Daniel held the door for her.

Bernie wove her way to a booth in the back. "They have good burgers, and when it comes to ice cream sundaes and shakes, this is the best place in town."

"Sounds like you speak from experience." He retrieved a menu from behind the napkin container. "What do you like?"

"Chocolate, of course. They only have the standards, but they're all good." She looked at him. "Wait. Don't tell me. Let me guess. You like strawberry shakes."

"No." He laughed. "I'm allergic to strawberries. I love caramel anything."

"Hi, Bernie. Hi, Doc." The little brown-haired waitress grinned at them. "Are you hungry or here for something sweet?"

Hi Doc? Bernie narrowed her eyes.

"Ice cream, Molly." Daniel gave her a warm smile.

"Super. The usual for both?" She raised her eyebrows, pencil poised to jot their order down.

"Sure." Bernie formed icicles on the word. Luckily, Molly didn't notice.

But Daniel did. His smile faltered.

72

After Molly walked away, Bernie folded her arms. "The usual? I thought you hadn't been here before?"

He spread his arms wide on the table. "I didn't want to spoil it. You were so excited and—"

"I don't like being lied to, whether directly or by omission." She raised her hand and drew in some slow, steady breaths. After a minute, she folded her hands on the table. "And I've been getting that a lot from you lately."

"I know." A muscle in his jaw twitched. "I lied about the gun."

She crossed her arms on the table. "Go on."

"I had a backup at home." He held up a finger. "Before you get upset, let me explain."

Their desserts came, but she pushed hers aside. "I want to know now."

"In Cleveland, I was involved with a colleague at work. Normally, we left together because the hospital isn't in the best of neighborhoods. One night, she wanted to go home, but I had work to do, so I let her leave alone. She was attacked and killed in the parking lot. I blame myself."

He gulped some water. "Ever since, I've been armed at all times. Ready to help anyone who might need it." He dug a spoonful of ice cream out of his bowl and let it drop. "I have a license for each gun."

"How many do you have?"

"Just the two."

"I'll need to see your backup to confirm it hasn't been fired." Bernie hoped he'd told her the truth, but she should be able to confirm his story with a few keystrokes. Why hadn't his other gun permit popped when she researched the first one?

"I'm sorry about your friend. For what it's worth, it's not your fault. That falls squarely on the shoulders of the person who killed her." She sighed. "Your guns didn't keep you from being attacked, nor were you able to stop the guy when you chased after him. Most often, non-professionals just end up hurting themselves, so you might consider leaving your guns at home from now on." She grabbed her purse. "I need to go."

"I'll walk you out." He slid to the end of the booth.

"No." She needed time to sort this out. "Stay and finish your ice cream. I'll see you tomorrow." She sensed he'd twisted the truth again. Pain stabbed her stomach, and she turned to go, clutching her purse to stop from wincing.

"GOOD NIGHT, BERNIE." Molly waved and approached Daniel's booth. "Is she all right?"

"Duty calls. You know how it is, being a detective."

"Yeah. She worked hard to get that promotion." Molly picked up Bernie's bowl. "Would you like anything else, Doc?"

"No. I'll just finish this. Thanks." Daniel smiled at her. Once she'd left, he stopped eating. He hadn't fooled Bernie with that stupid story—even though there was a kernel of truth in it.

"Are you finished, Doc?" Molly's voice sounded next to him.

"Yes. I guess I had too much to eat earlier." He handed her his dish. After paying for both ice cream sundaes, Daniel strolled between the buildings to the back parking lot. His car sat in the shadows under a broken light. He paused. It hadn't been that way when he arrived. Two men dressed in black with ski masks charged out of the darkness. One grabbed Daniel and forced him face-first against his car, while the other remained in the shadows.

"Any weapons on you?" The man's breath smelled of onions and teeth in need of brushing. His hand found the gun in Daniel's waistband. "Naughty, naughty." He waved it in Daniel's face before shoving it into his own pocket.

"We have a message for you, O'Leary. It's real simple. Go back to Cleveland, where you belong." The man wrenched Daniel's arm further up his back. "Tell your boss we get the need to settle the score with Ghazzi. But this part of the state is our territory. Time for you to go back to your own. If you don't, someone you love may get hurt. Understand?" He yanked on his arm again. "I can't hear you."

"Yes," Daniel whispered. "I understand."

"Good." The man took Daniel's gun from his pocket and slammed it into the doctor's head.

"That's enough. Let's go," the other man said.

Daniel gave in to the darkness.

Luckily, he came to before being discovered. No more trips to the hospital in an ambulance, and best of all, Bernie didn't have to know. He struggled to his feet and leaned against his car for a moment. His fingers probed his scalp. Ouch. He couldn't keep getting knocked on the head like this, or his brains would be scrambled for good.

A look around confirmed it. They took his gun.

His knees buckled, and he braced his hands on the tarmac to keep from pitching forward. After a couple of deep breaths, Daniel pushed to his feet and got into his car. He pulled out his phone. Time to get in touch with his contact.

12

Bernie pushed through the doors to the precinct. Daniel O'Leary haunted her dreams and waking thoughts. No one in her life had ever affected her this way. She wanted to shake him, but at the same time, definitely not run into him.

Please, Lord, let him stay home today.

"Santos, over here." Jeannie motioned with both hands. "You need to see this. Bring that chair around so you can read the computer."

"Can I get some coffee first?" Everything was a rush with Jeannie.

"Fine." Jeannie rolled her eyes. "But hurry it up."

Five minutes to get a cup of coffee. What's the big deal? She slammed her cup under the spout, banged the lid down, and punched the button. A stream of clear hot water poured into her cup. She'd forgotten the coffee pod. Raising her face to the ceiling, Bernie closed her eyes and stood still for a moment. Then she retrieved her cup and began again.

She sat a steaming cup of black coffee next to Jeanie's hand before easing into her chair, hands wrapped around her mug.

"What took so long?" Jeannie's gaze landed on the cup at her side. "Oh. Thanks." She picked it up and pointed to the screen.

"The guys finished the background checks on all the people at the school, and some interesting things came up."

She scooted over, and Bernie leaned in.

"And that's not all. You know how we couldn't find anything on the internet about Tariq Ghazzi except for a Yellow Pages listing?"

Bernie nodded. "I thought that was really weird. Everybody's on the internet these days."

"Except terrorists."

Bernie jerked her chair closer, spilling coffee on her pants. "Ghazzi's a terrorist?"

"My contact at Homeland Security called him a Person of Interest." Jeannie swiveled to face her.

Bernie grabbed some tissues and blotted her leg. "What else did he say about Ghazzi?"

"He wouldn't tell me anything else, but that was enough for me."

"What's a man like that doing in Pleasant Valley?" Bernie threw the soaked tissues in the trashcan. "Is Homeland Security taking over our investigation?"

Jeannie shook her head. "I asked him if they wanted in, and he said that since Ghazzi was dead, they no longer cared. I told him I'd let him know what we found out, but he didn't seem to care about that either."

"That doesn't sound right to me. Usually, the *federales* are hot to get their noses into something like this."

"It gets better." Jeannie pointed to the screen. "Take a look at our English teacher, Henry Abbott."

Henry Matthew Abbott. Born in Cleveland, Ohio. Two sisters. Irene and Elsa. Parents deceased. Sister Irene killed in a raid on a suspected terrorist hideout. Moved to Pleasant Valley seven years before.

Bernie whistled. "Ghazzi and Irene may have known each other in Cleveland. Maybe Henry Abbott was part of the same group, and he and Ghazzi had a falling out. Or he killed Ghazzi in revenge for his sister."

"I'm not sure, but coincidences are for idiots. He's mixed up in this somehow."

"Why would Abbott wait so long to murder Tariq Ghazzi? For that matter, why would he work for him at the school all those years before deciding to kill him?" She pulled on her ear. "Does this mean we drop Daniel for the time being and concentrate on Abbott?" The surge of hope surprised her.

"No. He's hiding something, and my gut tells me he's part of this too." Jeannie jabbed a finger at her computer. "In the meantime, we need to have another talk with Mr. Abbott. In our house this time."

Possible terrorists in Pleasant Valley? What could they be doing here?

Bernie dialed St. Martin's Prep. "This is Detective Bernadette Santos of the Pleasant Valley Police Department. We need to speak to Mr. Henry Abbott."

"I'm afraid Mr. Abbott has taken some vacation time," Ms. Pidgeon said. "He won't be back to work for a week."

"Did he indicate if he planned to stay in town?"

"I'm not permitted to give out that information."

Bernie closed her eyes. "Ms. Pidgeon. I understand your reluctance to give me any personal information you may have, but this is a murder investigation—the murder of your boss."

"The truth is, I really don't know," Ms. Pidgeon said, her arrogant tone now timid. "You don't think Henry had anything to do with Philip's murder, do you?"

"Thank you for your help." Bernie hung up. She entered his name into her computer and punched in his cell number. No answer. Voicemail. She had a bad feeling about this. After noting his address, she grabbed her jacket. "Jeannie, Mr. Abbott has taken a week off after we told him to stay put, and he isn't answering his phone. Time for a little visit, don't you think?"

"Yep." Jeannie closed her computer and adjusted her gun on

her waistband. "Let's go see what he's up to." Bernie led the way to their police-issued Dodge Charger.

Several minutes later, they stopped in front of a modest ranch-style home on the outskirts of town. Clean white siding wrapped the house on the three visible sides. Black shutters framed the windows with redwood planters beneath. Each held mums in brilliant autumn colors. It certainly didn't look like the home of a terrorist. The driveway was empty, and the drapes were drawn tight.

"Looks like no one's home." Jeannie rang the bell, and after a moment, pounded on the front door. "Mr. Abbott. Pleasant Valley Police. We'd like to talk to you."

Bernie peered through a gap in the curtains. "Just a couch and chair." She started around the corner of the house.

A woman in jeans and a T-shirt stepped out of the house to the right.

"May I help you?" She crossed her arms, her hand clutching a cell phone.

Bernie smiled and started her way. "We're looking for Mr. Abbott." She held her badge for the woman to inspect. "You don't happen to know where we might find him?"

"We don't talk much." She relaxed, but her fingers remained wrapped around her phone. "I saw him packing his car a couple of mornings ago."

"Like he was going on a trip?"

She nodded.

"What kind of car does he drive?" Bernie said.

"A black Lexus. I don't know the year, but it looks new."

Bernie noted the information on her phone. "What else can you tell me about Mr. Abbott?"

"Nothing, really. I only see him coming and going." She shrugged. "We just say hello and talk about the weather."

"Does Mr. Abbott ever have any visitors or bring anyone home with him?" Jeannie displayed a photo of Tariq Ghazzi on her phone. "Like this man, maybe?"

The neighbor peered at the picture. "I've never seen anyone here." She handed the phone back to Jeannie. "But I don't make it my business to snoop on my neighbors."

"Thanks. You've been very helpful." Jeannie nodded at Bernie.

They turned to go.

"Did he do something?" the woman said. "I mean. Am I living next door to an ax murderer or something?"

"We can't discuss—"

"No. Nothing like that." Bernie glared at Jeannie. She handed the woman a card. "We would appreciate a call if you see him."

Back in their car, Bernie rounded on Jeannie. "What was that all about? Are you trying to get us in trouble?"

Jeannie put out a BOLO on Henry Abbott and his Lexus. "Whatever happened to nosy neighbors? Used to be, we could count on the people living next door to know all the dirt."

"That's no reason to infer that her neighbor may be an ax murderer." Bernie adjusted her seat belt. "It's different now. I'm not sure I'd even recognize all my neighbors." She checked the mirrors. "What next?"

"We wait and hope someone spots his car."

When Bernie pulled into the police parking lot, she spied Daniel's red Infiniti, and her spirits plummeted.

"Are you going to sit out here all day and mope?" Jeannie stood with hands on her hips. "I don't know what's going on with you two, but you better get over it. And fast. I need your full attention, Santos."

Was it that obvious? Bernie squared her shoulders. She hadn't worked so hard to get to detective to mess it up over a man.

Bernie stopped by the breakroom for a coffee before going to her desk. No sign of Daniel. Good. She knew she couldn't avoid him forever, and sometime she had to see about his backup weapon. But not right now.

Jeannie gestured to her. "Abbott's on the phone."

She threw her cup in the trash and jogged over to Jeannie's desk.

"Mr. Abbott. Thanks for calling." Jeannie hit speaker.

"I heard your message. What's the problem?" A car horn sounded in the background. "We'd like to speak to you in person if possible. Where are you?"

"I'm at a B&B in Indiana."

Bernie frowned at Jeannie. Where in Indiana? It's a big state.

"We need you back in town. It's important we talk as soon as possible." Jeannie withdrew a notebook from the top drawer of her desk.

"Regarding what?"

"Some new information has come to our attention, and we need your help."

For several minutes all they could hear was the sound of traffic. Had he changed his mind about talking to them?

"Mr. Abbott?"

"I'm here." He sighed. "I guess you found out I knew Philip before—in Cleveland."

"Yes." Jeannie gave Bernie a thumbs up. "We're having trouble getting a handle on what happened to him. We think the answer may lie in his past. You could be a big help to us."

Bernie held her breath. Abbott could hang up, and then there would be a manhunt across state lines. Which meant the Feds would get involved. Or he could cooperate. Which would it be?

"I'll leave as soon as I can. It'll take me about three or four hours to get back. And I need to go home and check on my cat first."

"Who was taking care of your cat when you planned to be gone a week?"

"You called the school?"

"That's where we expected to find you." Jeannie leaned back in her chair. "Come directly here."

"But—"

"Now."

◄◆————————————◆►

ONE MINUTE the seat across from Daniel in the Main Street Diner was empty. The next, his informant was there. Dressed in shades of gray from his cap to his pants. Medium stature. No visible marks or tattoos. Even Daniel's trained eyes couldn't pick up anything. The man was very good at fading into the woodwork.

"I have the information you requested." With gloved hands, he withdrew several small, folded sheets of paper and slid them across the table.

"On all the major players?" Daniel scooped them up in a fluid motion and put them in an inside jacket pocket.

The man nodded.

"Is there any way I can count on you if I need backup?"

"No. Sorry. Only info." He glanced briefly at Daniel. "You understand."

Daniel nodded. He turned to where the waitress approached with his hamburger. When he looked back, the man had disappeared. He felt inside his jacket pocket for the papers he'd just received.

13

After two hours at the computer, Bernie pushed away from her desk and stretched. "I'm going outside to call my dad." She propped against the left fender of the car and pulled out her phone. She dreaded the upcoming interview with Henry Abbott and what it might reveal.

"Giving me the cold shoulder?" Daniel's voice sounded behind her.

She stiffened. Had he followed her from the building?

"Burr. More like icy."

She whirled around and let him see her anger.

"Bernie, please. I like you—a lot. Can we try to find a way to be friends?"

"In other words, will I just accept your lies and ignore them?" She glared at him.

"If I could tell you the whole truth, I would." He put his hand over his heart. "But I can't. I have a good reason, and I'm asking you to trust me."

She searched his blue eyes, and for once, realized he was telling her the truth. But what good reason could there be? "Did you kill Ghazzi?"

"Is that what you think?" He stepped away from her.

"I—You're mixed up in this somehow. I just wish I knew how." She massaged her temple. "I want to trust you. I really do."

"Can you at least try?" He touched her arm. "I didn't kill him."

The tone in his voice tugged at her heart. A black Lexus pulled into the lot, and Henry Abbott got out. She turned to leave.

Daniel tightened his grip on her arm. "Who's that?"

"A teacher at Major's—Tariq's—school." She pulled away. "I have to go."

"We'll talk later?" Daniel said.

"Okay." Bernie followed Abbott into the building. She caught up to him as Jeannie ushered him into an interview room.

"Glad you could make it, Detective." Jeannie glanced at her.

Bernie's face warmed.

WHILE JEANNIE and Bernie were preparing to interview Abbott, Daniel slipped into the viewing room.

"I've never seen a real interrogation before. Is it okay if I watch?" He gave the female technician his warmest smile.

"I don't know, Doc." She grimaced. "Authorized personnel only and all that."

Daniel sighed. "I understand. All this is just so fascinating to me. I promise not to tell if you won't. I won't stay long."

"Well, your aunt is the coroner, after all." She bit her lip. "I suppose it would be okay. But if anyone else comes in, you'll—"

"Of course." He turned his attention to the conversation in the room beyond playing on the monitors. Henry Matthew Abbott. Daniel recognized him. One of Ghazzi's insurance clients. Along with his sister, Irene. Only she was more than a client. Daniel remembered the day she died. He was at the raid that morning but wore a mask to protect his identity. Could

Abbott be one of the men who attacked him last night? His build didn't seem quite right, but it was possible.

Daniel focused in on the conversation.

Abbott was nervous. His arms wrapped tightly around his waist, and his left foot bounced on the floor. The heel of his shoe made a rapid tapping noise.

"Let's get right to it." Jeannie positioned her chair until her knees almost brushed Abbott's. She opened a file. "How were you acquainted with Mr. Majors in Cleveland?"

"I knew him by another name, Tariq Ghazzi." He pressed his back against the chair. "In the beginning, he was my insurance agent." Abbott rubbed his throat. "Could I have some water?"

"I was right," Daniel said under his breath.

"Pardon me?" the tech said.

"Nothing. Sorry." Daniel gave her a brief smile. He turned his attention back to the scene playing out in the room next door. Bernie was talking.

"You said in the beginning. What do you mean by that?"

"The man seduced my sister." Abbott took a drink. "He got her involved with some unsavory people."

"Irene?" Jeannie angled forward. "The one killed in the raid?"

An image flashed through Daniel's mind. A young woman disfigured by gunfire.

On the monitor, Abbott nodded.

"Did you get involved with those 'unsavory people' as well?" Bernie said.

"No." Abbott recoiled as if he'd been offered poison. "I did everything I could to get her away from him—and them." He bent forward. Deep furrows appeared on his brow, and his cheeks sagged, aging him ten years.

Bernie pulled her chair closer. "But you still worked for him here. Why?"

"At first, I didn't recognize him. He'd changed his appearance just enough, and, of course, his name was different." Abbott unfolded his body and clasped his hands in front of him.

Bernie made a quick note on her phone.

"By the time I realized who he was, well, jobs aren't that easy to come by, and I happen to like it here. I decided to put the past behind me and carry on."

Either Abbott was naïve, or he thought the detectives were idiots.

"Are you sure you weren't just waiting for the perfect moment to take a big rock and cave his skull in?" Jeannie kept her tone conversational. "I know I would if someone had done that to my sister."

Abbott winced. "I hated him, but I couldn't kill him. I wouldn't kill him."

Somehow, his words rang true. But why wouldn't he kill a man he hated?

"What do you mean? You had motivation."

"I just wouldn't." Abbott gave a wry laugh. "If anything, he'd be the one killing me. Unless you have something to charge me with, this interview is over, and from now on, you can talk to my attorney."

At the word "attorney", Daniel left the viewing room. "I need to be going. Thanks for letting me stay."

14

"Just one more question, please. Not about Ghazzi," Bernie
said.

Abbott glared at her. "What is it?"

"Did you know a man named Daniel O'Leary in Cleveland?"
Sweat trickled between her shoulder blades.

"No." He pushed his chair back against the wall and stomped
across the floor. He paused with one hand on the door. "Hang
on. That name does ring a bell."

Bernie tightened her grip on her papers. The sinking feeling
returned to her stomach.

"Isn't he a doctor or something? Got shot at a couple of
times? Is he from Cleveland too?"

"Thank you, Mr. Abbott." Bernie released the breath she'd
been holding. "Don't leave town again. We will have more
questions for you later."

"Only with my lawyer present."

After Henry Abbott left, Jeannie shuffled her files together.
"What do you think?"

"I think I'm tired of being told half-truths. Abbott says he
wouldn't kill Ghazzi, but won't give us a reason." Bernie rose.
"What a load of nonsense."

"He's got motive for killing Phillip Major, or Tariq Ghazzi, or whoever he was." Jeannie stood and held the door for her partner. "Revenge for his sister. Being passed over for the deanship at the school. And I'm sure we can find a few others if we dig."

The women walked in silence back to their desks.

"Still, I don't think he did it." Bernie loosened her ponytail and ruffled her hair. "I think he's guilty of something, but not murder."

"Have you gotten the vic's bank records yet?"

"You should be getting them now." She hit *send* on her computer. "Ghazzi had a hefty bank account. Where the initial balance came from, I have no idea. We'd need to go back further than his time in Pleasant Valley to find that."

Jeannie peered at the columns of numbers on her screen. "I see a regular withdrawal every month of five thousand dollars."

Bernie highlighted the transactions Jeannie mentioned. "That's a lot of money. Blackmail?"

"Possibly." Jeannie rubbed her eyes. "Maybe that's why our Mr. Abbott wouldn't have killed Ghazzi. He was Henry's cash cow."

"If that's the case, we need to search Henry Abbott's house right now and find out what he had on Ghazzi that was worth that much to him," Bernie said.

"I'll call for a warrant." Jeannie jumped up. "While we wait, I'm getting something to eat. Want to come?"

<hr/>

DANIEL WASN'T TAKING any chances. He texted his aunt that he needed to run some errands and would be back later. Once in his car, he saw Henry Abbott drive away in his black Lexus. Tailing anyone in a fire-engine red car was next to impossible, and not for the first time, Daniel wished he'd made a more sensible choice.

Maybe Abbott would be too shaken by his interview to notice him. Daniel managed to follow him home. He passed the house, stopped half a block away, and surveyed the neighborhood. When a garage door opened across the street, Daniel decided he'd seen enough and pulled away from the curb.

———

JEANNIE INSISTED ON DRIVING. Bernie shuddered, but they made it to Henry Abbot's house without incident. Abbott's car sat in his driveway. The rest of the team hadn't arrived.

An alarm sounded in Bernie's head. The door to his house stood ajar. No need for a warrant now.

Weapons drawn, they approached the car from two sides and glanced in the windows. Empty.

At a nod from Jeannie, Bernie moved to the open front door, her back to the wall. She cocked her gun arm and braced the fingers of her right hand with those of her left. Jeannie mirrored her position with the door between them. They looked at each other. Jeannie gestured a go-ahead.

Bernie crouched and brought her gun out in front of her. She eased the door open. "Pleasant Valley Police. We're coming in. Mr. Abbott? Are you in here?" At the sound of a soft patter of feet to her left, she stepped in and swung her weapon in that direction. A large yellow cat squatted on the hardwood floor. Its green eyes stared in her direction. Small bloody footprints crisscrossed the floor. "I see his cat. It may be hurt."

"Got it." Jeannie touched her back to let her know she was in the house.

The door clicked shut.

"Mr. Abbott? Pleasant Valley Police. If you're in here, come out where we can see you."

The rooms were a mess. Furniture was overturned, drawers lay smashed atop their contents, and pillows bled their white fluff over everything. There was a tinge of something in the air.

Tuna fish? Bernie indicated she'd go left. She moved through the living room into the kitchen. Mr. Abbott was sprawled back in a chair at the table, a gaping hole in the top of his head.

"In here." She studied the blood pattern on the ceiling.

Jeannie stepped into the room from a hallway. "The rest of the house is clear." She gazed at the man, arms dangling by his side with a revolver on the floor under his right hand. "Suicide?"

"Looks that way." Bernie squatted next to the body, careful not to touch anything.

Jeannie frowned. "Something's not right." She inspected the body.

"The entry wound and powder burns are consistent with suicide."

"I know, but—" Jeannie stared, hands on hips.

A partially opened can of cat food had fallen and come to rest against a far table leg. The cat padded over to it, regarded them for a moment, and began eating, daintily picking pieces off the floor.

"I suppose we should stop him. Since it's evidence and all." Bernie glanced at the cat.

"Let him be. I don't think it'll make much difference." Jeannie reached for her cell phone. "We need to get Rose over here."

Jeannie and Bernie waited on the porch for the coroner.

Fifteen minutes later, Rose bustled up the lawn with Daniel in tow. "Ladies." She placed a steadying hand on Daniel's arm and donned booties. After putting on gloves and a paper gown, she entered the house. Jeannie followed her in.

Bernie crossed her arms against her torso. Maybe he'd get the hint and leave her alone. But no. She heard his footsteps on the boards behind her.

"Doesn't your aunt need you inside?"

"Not yet."

Out of the corner of her eye, she saw his hand hover over her arm before dropping to his side.

"I haven't cared about anyone—"

"All right, you two. Enough of that." Rose barreled through the door with Jeannie on her heels. "Not a suicide, I'd guess."

"You're suggesting murder?" Bernie said, relieved for the interruption and somehow disappointed at the same time. What was Daniel about to say?

"His watch, pet. That great glorious gold monstrosity he wore on his right wrist." Rose tapped her hand. "I'm betting he was left-handed."

"Of course." Jeannie snapped her fingers. "I noticed that when he wrote his co-worker's number for me at the interview."

Rose nodded. "Most likely would have used his dominant hand, and the gun would have been found on the left side, wouldn't it?" She threw her gloves into a bag. "Someone wanted him dead."

"Why?" Jeannie said.

"That's your business, love. I'm just the lowly coroner, remember?" Rose motioned to her nephew. "Time for us to go. We have work to do."

Bernie and Jeannie stood shoulder to shoulder on the porch when the theme from *Mission Impossible* sounded from Jeannie's pocket.

"Jansen." She straightened her shoulders. "Yes, sir, we do have another murder." Jeannie glanced at Bernie. "She's doing a fine job, sir. There's no doubt in my mind that she's up to the task." Another pause. "Yes sir, we will, sir." Jeannie punched *End* and sighed.

"Acting Captain Yancy?" Bernie said.

Jeannie nodded. "He's concerned about two murders so close together and what our citizens will think."

"The press is giving him grief."

"That would be my guess." Jeannie dropped her phone into her jacket pocket. "Oh, and he questioned whether a new detective should be working on these cases."

"I gathered that. Thanks for sticking up for me."

Jeannie faced her. "I stuck my neck out for you because I believe you're good at this job. So, let's get to it. Someone found out Henry Abbott was blackmailing Ghazzi. What did he have that was so important?"

"We have to prove the theory first." Bernie swiveled to look at the house. "If blackmail is the motive, maybe they didn't find what they were looking for." She pushed off the railing. "Let's go see."

15

Rose heaved herself into the passenger seat and glanced back at Henry Abbott's house.

"We'll do this autopsy right away when we get back." She squeezed hand lotion onto her palm. "None of our other patients are as critical."

Daniel chuckled and started the van. "Do all coroners call their bodies patients?"

"And what would you have me call them? Cadavers? Corpses? Remains?" She tossed her tube of lotion into her bag.

"I apologize." He took one hand off the wheel and placed it on his heart. "I didn't mean to upset you."

"It's okay, boy. But these are not bodies to me. They're people, and when they meet a violent end like Mr. Abbott, I feel an obligation to help find their killer."

Daniel glanced at her. How much did his aunt know? Why were Jeannie and Bernie at Abbott's house in the first place?

"You should be a detective. You picked up on the watch. Even Jeannie didn't see that one."

Rose smiled. "Well, she's a smart one, that girl. She would have figured it out eventually. But I did save them some time."

She adjusted her seatbelt. "Now she and Bernie can get on with their search of the house."

"Search?" His hands tightened on the steering wheel.

"I was told they think Mr. Abbott was blackmailing Mr. Master—Ghazzi—whatever his name was. It would help to know what he had on the man." She sighed. "I suppose now that's another dead end. So to speak."

"Aunt Rose. Did you just make a joke about death?"

"In my business, you have to have a sense of humor, or you'll go crazy." She waved her hand at him and turned to the passenger window. "Sometimes, I think I'm already there."

Daniel backed the van into a space by the morgue doors and ran around to open the car door for his aunt.

"A girl could get used to this. I'm going to miss you when you start your job at the hospital."

Ah, yes, the hospital. He felt a brief stab of conscience. He retrieved her case from the van and followed her to her office. If Abbott was blackmailing Ghazzi, it could only mean one thing. Abbott knew what Daniel knew. But how? And, if Jeannie and Bernie found the evidence they sought, soon they would know as well. Then there'd be no reason for him to keep secrets from his aunt or Bernie. That would solve a lot of his problems.

"Daniel, what are you doing? Give me my case." Rose snapped her fingers.

Daniel blinked. "Sorry. Thinking of something else for a moment there."

"She wouldn't have wavy dark brown hair and deep brown eyes, would she?" His aunt gave him a sly grin.

"Stop playing matchmaker." Daniel took off his jacket. "I'm a grown man and can mess up a relationship on my own. Believe me."

"That's what I'm afraid of, boy." Rose slipped into her lab coat.

AFTER SEVERAL HOURS of searching Henry Abbott's house, Bernie and Jeannie returned to their police car.

Jeannie wiped her hands on a towel and threw it in the backseat. "Look at me. I'll need a change of clothes before I do anything else." She eyed Bernie's navy-blue pants. "Why do you look so clean?"

"I borrowed a pair of Tyvek coveralls from the crime scene techs."

"Why didn't you get me a set?"

"Because you waded into the mess before I could stop you."

"Story of my life." Jeannie threw an evidence bag on the back seat. "At least this one cleans up easily. That hasn't always been the case."

"Do you want to stop by your place on the way?"

"No. I've got extra clothes at the precinct."

Thankfully, Bernie was driving. The mood Jeannie was in, who knew if they'd make it back alive—or more likely, anyone crossing the street could be in real danger.

"Glad we have something to show for our efforts."

"Yeah. It's not much, a book of poetry and a photo of a group of kids. One who looks like it could be Ghazzi." Jeannie glanced behind her. "If there's anything, the guys in research can find it."

Back at the station lot, Jeannie hustled toward the building, but Bernie took her time, reluctant to encounter Daniel again. Her stomach clenched. She liked things black and white. Right and wrong. He blurred her boundaries. And that made her mad.

Inside, Bernie glanced down the hall toward the autopsy rooms. She balled her hands into fists and looked around for something to hit. The candy machine. *Wham.* Bad idea. She grimaced and shook her hand. A familiar sound caught her attention. Her favorite chocolate bar lay in the tray.

"When you're done roughing up the machine, meet me at my

desk." Jeannie hustled past, freshly clothed and carrying a bundle in her arms.

Bernie followed after her opening her candy bar. *Thank You, Lord, and sorry about that tantrum a minute ago.*

"Do we have any results from the house to house?" Jeannie dropped into her chair and stuffed her dirty garments into her bottom drawer.

"I'll check." Bernie used a tissue to wipe the chocolate from her fingers and punched the keys on her computer. Her throat closed up. "A woman reported seeing a red sports car outside her home earlier today, along with some other activity at Abbott's house." Oh, Daniel. Not again.

"Let's roll, partner." Jeannie grabbed her purse.

Bernie couldn't remember anything about the drive back to Abbott's neighborhood. For the second time in her life, she operated on unstable ground, unsure of herself. Her mind pulled her one way, while her heart yanked her another.

"Don't tell me you're getting a feel for the neighborhood again?" Jeannie's voice cut through her fog.

"No. I'm ready." She needed to follow her intellect, not her heart. She got out, straightened, and walked with Jeannie up the driveway.

At the door, Jeannie rang the bell. No answer.

She glanced at Bernie. "Mrs. Nayar? Pleasant Valley Police." Jeannie pounded on the door. "We have a few questions."

After a minute, the door opened to a large, muscular man in jeans and a T-shirt. "My wife is not home." He spat the words.

Bernie couldn't place his accent. But the name indicated somewhere other than the U.S. Perhaps India or the Middle East.

As he pushed the door shut, Jeannie blocked it with her hand.

"When will she be back? We need to speak with her about what she saw yesterday."

"Where are your credentials?"

Jeanie and Bernie yanked them out.

He studied them before handing them back.

"It was a mistake." He glared at Jeannie. "She saw nothing. She has nothing to tell you."

This time, he managed to close the door before Jeannie could do anything to stop him.

Back in the car, Bernie studied the house. "I know I saw a figure behind the living room curtain. I don't think he wants her to talk to us."

"Since when has that stopped me?" Jeannie drove off but pulled over a block away. "Now, we wait."

After twenty minutes, the garage door opened, and a brown sedan backed out.

Bernie turned as the car passed them—a woman in the driver's seat. "That's got to be her."

The detectives trailed her to a nearby shopping center and watched as she pushed a cart into the grocery store.

After five minutes, Jeannie nodded. "Let's go in."

They found her in the canned vegetable aisle. She was lost in thought, gazing at the sweet potatoes and reaching for her selection.

Bernie stepped up behind her. "Mrs. Nayar?"

The poor woman screeched and dropped to a crouch with her arms above her head.

Bernie touched her elbow. "We're not going to hurt you. We just want to talk. Please."

Both detectives displayed their badges.

She straightened, her lean body trembling. "I can't talk to you. Go away. I have to get my shopping done." She grabbed two cans and threw them into her cart. "I cannot be late getting home." She pushed her sunglasses up her nose and turned from them. A faint discoloration showed on the cheekbone under her left eye.

"What happened?" Bernie put a hand on her cart. "Did your husband hit you?"

Tears slid down smooth olive-colored skin. "He was so mad. He hates the police." She buried her face behind slender fingers.

"If you tell us what you saw, we promise to investigate it without bringing you into it," Jeannie said.

Bernie stared at her partner. Why had she made a promise she couldn't keep?

"You can do that?" Mrs. Nayar lowered her hands.

Jeannie nodded.

Bernie couldn't believe it. "Unless—"

"Unless you decide later to come forward. That would be best for all of us." Jeannie gave her a gentle smile. "Until then, what you say is just between us."

"I saw a red sports car parked across the street," Mrs. Nayar whispered. "When I opened my garage door to leave for the post office—Kabir had some packages ready to mail—the car left. As I backed onto the street, a white pickup turned into Mr. Abbott's driveway." She leaned toward them. "That is all. Now, I beg you, let me go. If I do not return home soon, my husband will question my delay."

The detectives stepped back.

"Thank you, Mrs. Nayar. You've been a big help," Jeannie said.

Bernie handed her a card. "There's help in this country for women who are hit by their husbands. Call me."

A tear slid from beneath her dark glasses. "It is too late, Detective. The devil took my husband's heart. And mine also."

16

Outside the grocery store, Bernie paused. Mrs. Nayar was the second person to allude to the devil. She slipped her hand into her pants pocket and skimmed her fingers across her medallion. She'd known some devils in her time. One in particular—the man she almost married. They could be oh so charming until ... But this was different. Mrs. Nayar didn't say Kabir was a devil—she said the devil took his heart.

"I think it's time to get Bulldog involved." Jeannie joined her.

Bernie started. "What?"

"Come on. I'll introduce you."

"Where are we going?" Bernie jogged after her partner.

"Back to the precinct." Jeannie jumped in the car and turned the key. "Buckle up."

No need to remind her. Wonder if the police garage would install one of those harnesses like the race car drivers had in their cars?

Once inside the station house, Jeannie led Bernie down a hall and through a door marked Research. Two women and a man peered in concentration at computers. Jeannie marched over to the man and pulled the plug on his headphones.

"Hey." He rolled away and removed his earphones all in one

motion. When he spotted Jeannie, he groaned. "I should have known it was you, Jansen. I haven't had a chance to work on your stuff yet."

"Nice to see you too, Randy." She stepped aside. "First, I want you to meet Detective Bernadette Santos."

"It's nice to meet you." He smiled and offered his hand. "I'm Randy Ingersoll, but everybody calls me Bulldog."

"You can call me Bernie." She laughed.

"Okay, enough of the formalities stuff," Jeannie said. "We need your help on something else involved with the same case. Number one, we need a list of all the owners of white pickups in Pleasant Valley and the surrounding area. Go out to county lines."

She held up two fingers. "Two, we need everything you can find on Kabir Nayar and his wife, Amber. In particular, we're looking for any connection to our dead guys, Philip Major/Tariq Ghazzi, and Henry Abbott." She lowered her hand. "Got that?"

"Yep. When do you need it?"

"Yesterday." Jeannie chuckled.

"I do have other people's requests ahead of you."

Jeannie bent over him. "But they don't get you season tickets to FC Cincinnati, do they?"

He shook his head and squared his chair to his desk. "I'll get on it right away."

"Thanks, Bulldog."

In the hallway outside of Research, Jeannie charged off out of sight. Bernie waited to see how long before she realized her shadow wasn't there.

After a moment, Jeannie stuck her head around the corner. "What gives? We have work to do."

Lord, give me strength. "I'm not sure I can work with you any longer." Bernie stiffened.

"If you're talking about what happened in there ..." Jeannie came closer. "You don't have the whole story." She waved her hand toward the Research door. "Things aren't always what they seem."

"It's not just that. It's—" Bernie shook her head.

New to the job, how much should she say about what was upsetting her? How could she know what was normal? Should that matter, anyway? Or had she chosen the wrong profession?

Jeannie eyed her. "How about a break in the canteen, and we can talk?"

Inside the canteen, they found a booth in the corner.

"You said I didn't have the whole story. What did you mean?"

"I promised Randy I'd never tell, but I have a gut feeling I can trust you." Jeannie took a deep breath. "A year back, he got himself into a pickle. Gambling. I bailed him out." She pressed her lips together before continuing.

"There was no way he could ever pay me back. So, he pledged to make my stuff first priority whenever I came to him. I try not to abuse it, but when I need it, I need it. Today, I used the season-ticket thing to remind him of our agreement."

"I owe you an apology for that one." Bernie steeled herself. "But what about promising Mrs. Nayar to investigate Abbott's murder without bringing her into it? You lied to that woman."

"I didn't lie." Jeannie glared at her. "I don't intend to bring her into it. I'll find another way to get the information into the investigation. She has enough problems."

Bernie studied her partner's face. "Was Ms. Pidgeon's drawer ajar?"

"No, that was me getting out of bounds." Jeannie looked away. "And, I'm sorry." She leaned forward. "Look. I think we're good together. I'm action and have connections, but sometimes I go too far. You're the brains and keep me honest." She bit her lip. "But if you want another partner, I'll understand."

Jeannie made Bernie's head spin. Fast-paced, quirky, rough around the edges. But a good heart.

"I don't want another partner. You're the best there is. I know I can learn a lot from you." She touched her pocket. "But

you need to listen to me when I tell you you've crossed the line."
Bernie paused. "Now, the question is, do you still want to be
partners with me?"

"You bet." Jeannie thumped the table, then glanced around
the canteen. "Of course, you're not going to like what comes
next."

———————————————

JEANNIE WAS RIGHT. Once more, Bernie found herself seated in
Interview Room 2 with Daniel. But this was a Daniel she hadn't
seen before. His twinkling blue eyes had turned to ice, and the
easy smile was lost in his clenched jaw muscles.

"I'm not the only one with a red car."

"You're right." Jeannie selected a sheet of computer paper
with a list on it. "There are a hundred in the area. Of course,
thirty are owned by fire stations, fifty are four-door sedans built
before 2010, and ten more were out of town at the time, and
they weren't what would be called sporty." She squinted at the
paper. "That leaves ten possibilities.

"Five are Mustangs—a pretty distinctive model. One is a
Corvette, which most people recognize. Now we're down to
four." Jeannie drew a photo of a red Infiniti from the pile.
"Looks pretty sporty to me. I wonder if the witnesses who saw it
would recognize it?" She laid it before Daniel on the table.
"What do you think, Doc?"

He crossed his arms.

Bernie blinked back the tears forming behind her eyes. He
was lying again. She saw it in his eyes. But why? She didn't
believe he killed Abbott. But he might have seen something that
could help with the case.

"Can I go now?" He scraped his chair across the linoleum
floor.

Jeannie waved him away. When the door had closed, Bernie
uncapped her water and took a swig.

"He's lying. Again." Bernie hated dishonesty in a man. Somehow, she needed to divorce herself from personal feelings and look at the case, the man, objectively. The academy classes hadn't prepared her for the real thing.

"Something's going on, and it's driving me crazy." Jeannie yanked on her ponytail. "Got any ideas?"

"Why would he have been outside Abbott's house?"

"He killed Abbott."

"Besides that."

"Surveillance?" Jeannie picked up her pencil and wrote Daniel's name on her pad.

"But why?" Bernie said. "What if he's not a doctor? What if he's undercover?"

"For the good guys or the bad guys?"

Bernie shrugged. "I guess it's up to me to find out." But she'd need to guard her heart. She closed her eyes. *Lord, help me.*

17

"I realize my mistake." Daniel's voice echoed in the empty men's room. "That's beside the point."

"You brought the stupid car," the voice on the other end of the phone said. "I told you to drive a company car down—something black and inconspicuous—but no. Not you."

"Fine. You were right. I'm an idiot. Is that what you want to hear? I'm about to be arrested for murder. Are you going to help me or not?"

"What do you want me to do?"

Daniel outlined his plan and ended the call. He leaned on the sink and stared at his face in the mirror. The red Infiniti was her dream, not his. After he killed—after her death—he bought it as ... what? A memorial? But it was time to get rid of it. Let it go. He checked the corridor before ducking through the door and returning to autopsy.

"There you are, Danny." Rose smiled at him. "What did the lady Ds want?"

"Just a few more questions about the night Ghazzi was killed." He yearned to confide in the motherly woman beside him. But that would never do. "If we're done for the day, I'd like to go home. I'm beat."

"Of course. I'll clean up." She stripped off her gloves and laid a hand on his cheek. "Take care of yourself, love."

He covered her hand with his. "I'm trying. I love you." He needed to eat and about twelve hours of sleep.

Outside, Bernie leaned against his driver's side door. He inwardly moaned.

"I was hoping to catch you." She stood, fingers twisting her ring. "I want you to know I believe you."

"Thanks." He stopped a few feet away. "It means a lot."

"I'm finished for the day. Want to grab a burger or something?"

She had the worst timing. He sighed.

"I'm dead on my feet, Bernie." He shoved his hands into his pant pockets. "Could we—"

"That's fine." She sidestepped past him. "I totally understand. Another time."

He grabbed her arm and pulled her closer. That smell of lemons and warm cotton. He touched her hair and brought his hand to rest under her chin. Tilting her face upward, he opened his mouth to speak. Soft, full lips covered his in a firm kiss. Warmth flooded his body, but before he could react, she pushed him away.

"Sorry. I forgot. You're tired." She walked away and got in her car.

Bernie drove past him without a glance. Daniel's spirit sagged. What was he doing? He had no business getting involved with someone. He got in his car. Time to go home.

At the rental house, a car pulled away from the curb, opening a parking space outside his front door. Gathering a few things from the seat, he dragged himself across the lawn. At the door, he dropped his keys. When he bent to retrieve them, he noticed another note stuck under the mat.

This is your last warning. He flipped the note over, but that was all.

A high-pitched whistle filled the air. Daniel dove to the ground.

18

Daniel's red Infiniti flew through the air. Shock waves from the explosion set off car alarms along the entire block. Noise from the blast stunned his eardrums, and thousands of pieces of scorched car parts rained on everything within a 50-foot radius. A pall of gray smoke poisoned the air.

He sat, braced against the front of the house as neighbors appeared to help. And gawk. He lay back and closed his eyes, waiting for the approaching sirens. This wasn't the plan he'd discussed with his boss.

———————◇———————

It took all of Bernie's willpower not to look back at Daniel as she'd driven away. Her heart ached to believe him, and she told him she did. But did she? Had Daniel been outside Abbott's house? She remembered Daniel's hold on her arm, tightening when Abbott arrived at the station. Had he known Abbott in Cleveland before?

Why couldn't her mind and her heart unite behind him? She touched her lips. Her kiss contained the sincerity her words lacked. Tears blurred her vision. She pressed the accelerator and cranked up the radio volume, surrendering herself to the rhythmic Latin beat.

In her driveway, Bernie shut off her engine and let the stillness envelop her. Her father's car wasn't there. Dampness seeped through her blouse to her skin. Was she crying?

"This will never do, Detective Bernadette Santos." She swiped her hands across wet cheeks and opened the car door.

"Hello, beautiful." Squawk. "Time for a snack."

"You think so?" Bernie placed her hand against the soft green feathers. "Step up."

Lori Darling climbed her arm and nudged Bernie on the cheek. "Love you."

"Love you too. Crackers? Or peanuts?"

The parrot reached for a peanut with her beak.

"I wish Papá would call." Bernie grabbed a handful of peanuts and moved to the couch, the parrot still perched on her shoulder. She offered another nut to her feathered friend. "Today, I kissed a suspect. What kind of detective does that?"

"Give us a kiss." Lori touched Bernie's cheek.

"Thanks, sweet—"

The James Bond theme sounded from her phone.

Squawk. "007."

"Shhh." Bernie punched the green button.

"Somebody just blew up your boyfriend's car." Jeannie's excited voice yelled at her over the phone.

She couldn't speak. "Where?" When she managed to push the word out, her voice came in a whisper. "How is he?"

"I can barely hear you. He's okay. He wasn't in it. It happened just as he got home."

Tears streamed from Bernie's eyes unbidden and washed down her cheeks.

"I'll meet you at his place," Jeannie said.

Bernie gazed longingly at her living room. She yearned for

time to herself—time to understand her reaction. Time to decide how she truly felt about Daniel. But that would have to wait. She was needed at a crime scene.

"Sorry, Lori. Back to your cage."

As she wound her way through the streets of Pleasant Valley, she prepared herself for the sights and smells of a bomb site. Each one was different but never failed to affect her. The destruction, the debris, and the acrid smell of burning metal, fabric, and plastic. At least this one didn't have any dead bodies.

Jeannie and Daniel stood on the grass. Bernie parked among the other police cars. She straightened her jacket and strode to them.

"What a mess," she said. "I'm sorry about your car."

His hands were jammed in his pants pockets with his arms tight against his body. Something had changed. He avoided her gaze.

"Dr. O'Leary received a threatening note just before the incident." Jeannie handed Bernie a plastic evidence bag with a piece of paper inside. "What do you make of it?"

Last warning? What was going on here? Bernie thrust the note at Jeannie and peered at Daniel.

Her head throbbed. "I think ... we all need some rest."

Daniel relaxed his stance.

"I think Detective Santos is right," Jeannie said. "Can you stay with your aunt tonight? We'll put a squad car outside her place. That way we'll all sleep better." Jeannie tapped Daniel on the chest. "But first thing tomorrow, I want to see you in our office again. Got that?"

Daniel nodded and pulled his hands out of his pockets. "I'll call Aunt Rose."

◄──────────────►

WHEN BERNIE ARRIVED at work the next day, what seemed like a manuscript for a book lay in the middle of her desk. Upon closer inspection, it was a list of all the owners of white pickups within the county—10,323 names. She snorted. Unless she and Jeannie could narrow the list, this was a complete waste of time. And Jeannie would never agree to interviewing Mrs. Nayar again to see if she could help. She hefted the stack of paper and dropped it in her bottom drawer.

"I saw that." Jeannie materialized next to her. "Who knew so many people liked white trucks? I've got officers canvassing the neighborhood. We need to find someone else who noticed Abbott's visitor." She handed Bernie a cup of coffee. "But I'm not holding my breath."

Bernie blew on her coffee before taking a tentative sip. A shift in the atmosphere put her senses on high alert. Rose steamed through the door and forged a path straight for Jeannie. Judging by her grim expression, she wasn't there to chat.

"My nephew has been attacked, threatened, shot at, and had his car blown to smithereens. And not only have you failed to catch whoever's doing this, but you've treated him as if he's a criminal." She slammed her worn briefcase down on the corner of Jeannie's desk.

Jeannie flinched. "Rose—"

"Dr. O'Leary, to you, Detective Jansen."

Obviously at a loss for words, Jeannie motioned to the chair next to her desk.

After a long moment, Rose sat. She retrieved her briefcase and placed it in her lap.

"The truth is, there's not much to go on." Jeannie faced the irate woman. "Whoever's after Daniel isn't leaving behind any traces for us to follow. We have a sighting of a white sedan. Do you know how many of those there are around? And we have a man in a large hooded coat." She shrugged. "Where does that get us? Nowhere."

"So, the only thing we have to go on are the weapons used to attack him. Not your typical carry guns, and we have our people working on that angle." She lifted her chin. "As for treating Daniel as a suspect, you already know why that is, and you know it's not unreasonable."

"Yes." Rose's shoulders sagged. "But I've known him since he was born, and he's a good man. Despite his worthless father—my brother, I'm ashamed to say." She rubbed her eye. "His mother, my sister-in-law, is a saint. Why she married that *jackeen* is beyond me." She swallowed. "But there's no accounting for love, is there?"

She opened her briefcase and rifled through the contents, withdrawing a slim file and placing it on Jeannie's desk. "I told you I'd find out about brimstone." She huffed to her feet and pointed her finger at Jeannie. "You keep doing your job, Detective, and I promise I'll help you as much as I can."

"I will, Doctor O'Leary."

"You can call me Rose." She pivoted and caught sight of Bernie.

Uh oh.

"And you, young lady." She covered the distance to Bernie's desk in two strides. "Don't even think about breaking my nephew's heart—or you'll have me to contend with."

Bernie was still trying to formulate an answer when the imposing woman shifted her briefcase and stomped out. After the door swung shut on Rose, Bernie crossed to the chair by Jeannie's desk, the seat still warm from the M. E.

"What have we found out about the weapons used in the attacks on Daniel? Especially last night. How did the bad guys blow up his car?"

"Do you have any idea how many people have registered semi-automatic rifles in our county alone?" Jeannie opened her computer. "A lot." She picked up a pair of glasses and glanced at Bernie. "Walgreen's specials." After scrolling through several screens, she stopped. "Looks like a small shoulder-held missile was used on his car." She sat back.

"Who are we dealing with here?" Bernie leaned in to read the monitor.

"Terrorists?"

"In Pleasant Valley?" Bernie shook her head and picked up the folder on Jeannie's desk. "Let's see what Rose found out." She scanned the report. "The rock is granite with various metal sulfides mixed in—whatever that means. From traces found on the surface, forensics believe it came from a coal mine."

"Not much help." Jeannie blew out a puff of air. "Unless Daniel's undercover for the mining industry?" She chuckled. "Whaddya think? Maybe Ghazzi was really an industrial spy."

Bernie laughed. "Don't think so."

"Me neither." Jeannie propped her head in her hands and stared at her computer screen. "Anything else in that report?"

"Sulfur was found on the hearth, and a twenty-pound bag of fast-acting sulfur can be bought at any lawn care center."

"Another dead end. When are we going to catch a break?"

Bulldog—Randy Ingersoll—trotted up to the desk. "Am I good or what?" He flourished a handful of papers in front of Jeannie's nose. "I managed to identify three of the teenagers in the photo, and I have a hunch who the fourth one is."

She took them and began to read. "Tariq grew up around here? And he had a step-sister and-brother?"

"Yeah." Randy nodded. "That's Ghazzi on the left. On the right is Henry Abbott."

"Abbott?" Bernie threw him a quizzical look. "I thought he grew up in Cleveland."

"He did, but his maternal grandparents had a farm around here. They came down to visit in the summer."

"Who are the girls?" Jeannie said.

Randy bent over and pointed to the picture. "Abbott has his arm around Ghazzi's step-sister. I just know her nickname. Dove. I think the young girl may be Abbott's other sister—the one who wasn't killed. Her name was Elsa. That's the only one I'm not sure about."

Bernie picked up the book of poetry they took from Henry Abbott's home and opened the front cover. The words *Happy birthday. Love, E,* were inscribed on the inside. "Who's E?"

"Elsa?" Randy shrugged.

"We need to find Dove and Elsa. Now," Jeannie said.

"Already on it." He pointed to the stack of papers he'd given her. "You might like to read these too."

"You found Major's—Ghazzi's—files."

He pointed to the papers. "Look at the page—"

"Thanks, Bulldog, but I need to go through these my way." Jeannie passed the first page to Bernie.

This was it. The break they'd been looking for. Notes about indiscretions, firings, disagreements. Bernie looked at Jeannie, muttering to herself as her eyes devoured the words before her.

"Bulldog, you're a genius." Jeannie handed the second page to Bernie.

A series of emails covered the page. As Bernie read, she understood why Jeannie seemed so excited. Someone had sent Major/Ghazzi a string of increasingly threatening notes. The last simply said, 'I will see you rotting in the ground.'

"Do we know where these came from?" Bernie said.

Bulldog grinned and whipped a notecard from behind his back like a conjurer culminating a difficult magic trick. He laid it on the desk. "His name and address."

Both women peered at the name.

Kabir Nayar.

"Are you sure?" Jeannie said.

He nodded. "What's wrong?"

"It's unexpected. That's all." Bernie picked up the card and tapped it against her knuckles. "Good job." She frowned. "Have you found anything out about Nayar or his wife?"

"Some." He nodded to the papers scattered on Jeannie's desk. "I guess I'll get back to work. Is there anything else for now?"

"Jeannie?" Bernie looked at her partner.

"No. Thanks, Randy. Excellent work." Jeannie scribbled on a file. "We'll call if we need anything more."

After he'd gone, Bernie turned to Jeannie. "She may not have known. His wife, I mean."

"Yeah. Maybe not." Jeannie rose. "Either way, her life's going to change forever. I only hope it's for the good."

19

For the second time in two days, Bernie and Jeannie pounded on the Nayar's door. This time, they had their guns drawn, a handful of police officers behind them, and a warrant to search the premises.

A high-pitched voice answered their knock. "I have told you all I know, detectives. Now go away. Please."

Jeannie turned to Bernie. "You take the lead."

"We're here to see your husband, Mrs. Nayar. Let us in." Bernie lowered her weapon.

Sobs grew louder as Mrs. Nayar slowly opened the faded blue door. "He is not here."

"We'd like to check for ourselves," Bernie said.

"Do you have a warrant?"

"Yes, ma'am, but it would be better if you let us in. Please. It's important. It will only take a few minutes."

"Will I be arrested if I do not?"

"You could be." She mellowed her voice to soften the impact of her words. "And, we'd be forced to break down your door. We really don't want to do that."

They waited for what seemed like several minutes but was probably only seconds.

Mrs. Nayar stepped back for the two detectives and other police officers to enter.

Bernie paused to get her bearings. An exquisite oriental rug in shades of red and blue covered the entire floor in the modest living room. Soft music reached her ears with vocals in a foreign language. And the smells. She wrinkled her nose. Not unpleasant, but different. All these elements combined to transport her to another country by stepping over the threshold.

"Have a seat, Mrs. Nayar." Jeannie guided her to a low chair. "We need to take a look around."

She wiped her eyes and waved permission. The officers did a quick sweep of the simple three-bedroom ranch house.

A table in a corner of the living room held a picture of a young boy in his school uniform holding his clarinet. He was about ten years old. A crucifix and a candle stood next to the photo.

"Is your son at school, ma'am?"

The woman exploded from the chair, grabbed the frame from its place on the table, and collapsed to the floor. "My son is dead. The devil killed my angel, and now you want to take my husband as well."

"I'm sorry, Mrs. Nayar." Jeannie squatted by her side.

When the woman turned away, Jeannie gestured to a female police officer to take over.

A quick search revealed nothing of interest. A pile of men's work clothes, stained black, covered the floor in the tiny laundry room. The exotic aroma proved to be coming from a pot of stew bubbling on the stovetop. Two plates lay on the low table in the dining room. By the time they got back to the living room, Mrs. Nayar sat in the chair, clutching the photograph, but calm.

Bernie and Jeannie perched on the sofa across from her.

"I know this must be hard for you." Bernie took out her phone. "But can you tell us how your son died?"

"Deniz was on a school outing." She spoke softly and without looking up. "It was a special competition. Only five children were chosen." A tear spilled over onto her cheek. "It was an accident, they said. The driver did his best, but something on the van broke." She traced the image of her son on the glass. "Now, my angel is dead."

"Why did you say—"

Jeannie elbowed Bernie and drew a finger across her throat. "Again, we're sorry for your loss, Mrs. Nayar." She consulted her notes. "About your husband. Where does he work?"

"At the new coal mine to the north." She lifted swollen eyes to Jeannie's. "What has he done? Why do you need to see him?"

Bernie's pulse quickened. She glanced at Jeannie. Maybe they were finally getting somewhere. "When does he get off? Is he due home soon?"

The poor woman focused fearful eyes on Bernie.

"You're preparing a meal, and I saw the plates," Bernie said. "You might as well tell us."

"He will be home at noon." Mrs. Nayar trembled.

Jeannie stood. "I need to talk to you." She motioned to Bernie, and the detectives walked into the kitchen. "Considering what we know about this guy, we may have a fight on our hands, getting him down to the station for a talk. I'd rather Mrs. Nayar wasn't here when we confront him. What do you think?"

"I agree, but how do we do that legally?"

"I'm not sure." Jeannie leaned against the counter. "Do you think you could sweet talk her into it?"

"I can try." Bernie pulled on her lip. "But if it doesn't work, I think we have to let her stay."

They returned to the living room.

"Mrs. Nayar, I'd like you to come down to the station ahead of your husband to look at photos of cars and trucks to help us with our investigation. Would you be willing to do that?"

"Why can I not wait for Kabir? He will be home soon."

"Please, Mrs. Nayar, we're very anxious to have you see these photos. We believe we're close to finding out who killed Mr. Abbott. We'll bring Mr. Nayar to you as soon as he arrives."

"I wish to remain here." Her features hardened "Kabir will expect me." She huddled on the sofa, clutching her son's photo to her breast. "I will wait for him."

No go. Bernie glanced at Jeannie. They'd have to make the best of it.

She stepped outside and approached the sergeant. "Move all the cars out three blocks—including ours. I don't want anything spooking him."

"Got it." He nodded.

"We'll need two of your biggest guys with us in the house. The rest can be in their cars or hidden if you trust them to know how to stay out of sight." She glanced at her watch. "We need to get moving."

"I'll take care of it." The sergeant called across the lawn to two officers by a patrol car.

"I know you will. I'm glad you're here, John." She jogged back to the house. "Jeannie?"

"In here." Jeannie's called from the kitchen.

Bernie related what she'd told the men to do.

"Good."

The two police officers in full gear walked in.

"Santos, you take the front door, and I'll take the back. One of you take cover down the hall. The other stay with Mrs. Nayar. Let him get all the way in before saying anything. Be prepared for a violent reaction. But no guns—if you can help it. Let us take the lead."

Five minutes after twelve. Bernie lifted first one foot and then the other trying to maintain circulation. Every car that passed the house sent a frisson of anticipation through her body. Maybe Nayar had to work late. Would he call his wife? What should they do if the phone rang? Wouldn't he expect her to be home? Or maybe a neighbor saw the police and—

The distinctive sound of a key in a lock. An instant of alarm. She'd forgotten to lock the front door. Would he notice? Luckily, he was coming in the back. Bernie didn't dare move until she heard Jeannie's voice.

A door slammed. "Where are you, woman? Why are you letting my dinner get cold?"

Mrs. Nayar erupted from the sofa. "Kabir? I had to let——"

Mild oaths as the officer attempted to block her progress without restraining her. "Mrs. Nayar, please. Stay here."

Commotion in the kitchen. Slamming drawers. Loud footsteps.

"Mr. Nayar?" Jeannie's voice sounded from behind the wall.

A roar reached Bernie's ears as she ran for the kitchen. She skidded to a halt inside the narrow doorway, gun drawn. The officers converged behind her.

"Kabir, please. No trouble." Mrs. Nayar strained to get past the police officers cutting off the entrance to the kitchen.

"Be quiet, you silly woman," Kabir Nayar bellowed.

Jeannie pressed against the far wall, arms extended, and eyes focused on the large, angry man in front of her. "Mr. Nayar. We only want to talk."

"Police never want only to talk." Light flashed off the gleaming butcher knife in his hand.

"Drop the knife, or I'll be forced to shoot you." Bernie's gunsights filled with the soiled coveralls across the man's back. *Lord, please let him calm down.*

"Stupid woman, you won't shoot me. You'll hit your partner."

A numbness overtook her. Unless her aim hit him at the right spot, the bullet would go right through him and into Jeannie.

Kabir swung the knife at Jeannie, slicing her left forearm. He wrenched the door open and took off across the yard. The two officers pushed past Bernie and chased after him, followed closely by Amber Nayar.

"Grab that towel." Jeannie's voice cut through her haze.

Bernie helped her partner while she spoke into her radio. "Officer down."

"I got this." Jeannie gripped her wrapped arm with her other hand. "Go find that jerk before he hurts somebody else."

Bernie glimpsed the blood on the kitchen floor. "I can't leave you." What an idiot she'd been.

"Catching him is more important," Jeannie said, through gritted teeth. "It's only a flesh wound."

Police officers and EMTs rushed into the kitchen, nudging Bernie aside. But even then, she was reluctant to leave. How could she hope to catch up with the pursuit? Her radio crackled to life.

"We've got him cornered."

20

Some medical examiners liked listening to music as they worked, but not Rose. A police scanner was her preferred background noise. And Daniel was glad she did.

A familiar voice filled the autopsy room.

"Is that Bernadette?" Rose paused with a scalpel in her hand.

"Officer down." Bernie called for help over the radio.

Daniel stripped off his gloves and moved toward the exit.

"Where are you going?" Rose stared at him.

"Sorry. I guess I'm worried about her." It was second nature. In Cleveland, he'd be expected to respond. But this wasn't Cleveland. He pulled a new set of gloves from the box.

"It's okay, boy. Let's finish here, and then you can check on her." His aunt sighed. "I'm not so old that I don't remember young love."

He had a long way to go before he'd call it love. Although, she did kiss him like she meant it last night. But what his aunt saw was something else entirely. Urgent voices on the scanner pulled at his attention. The police were chasing a suspect. They had him surrounded.

Bernie's voice again. "Don't do anything. I'm on my way."

Who were they after? Was he the man who killed Ghazzi?

Daniel found it hard to concentrate on continuing with the autopsy. Finally, she pushed the microphone away and pulled off her gown and gloves.

"We're finished here. My assistant can do the rest." She waved a hand at Daniel. "Go on. Get out of here. I'll see you at home."

He stripped off his garments and remembered the extra hand-held police radio his aunt kept in her desk. He cracked the door to the woman's dressing room. The shower was running. In her office, he pulled on the bottom drawer. It wasn't locked. He removed the radio, slipped it into his jacket pocket, and left.

Inside the silver Honda Accord rental, Daniel let out a long breath. A mile away from the police station, he parked and tuned the radio into the police frequency. The runner was holed up at St. Martin's Prep. Daniel plugged the destination into the car's navigation system. Five minutes, and he'd be there.

The police set up a perimeter of three blocks surrounding the school, which was situated in an established neighborhood. Daniel crept close without being seen. Evacuated teachers and other school personnel gathered behind the police cars and vans. Bernie huddled with two women and gestured toward the school. One woman, tall and straight with gray hair. The other, about Bernie's height with brown hair.

A sudden sense of *déjà vu* swept through him. Daniel frowned. What triggered it? No time to figure it out. Bernie broke from the group. His radio crackled to life, and he turned the volume down to a whisper. Bernie wanted to enter the school from the back and talk to the man inside.

Jeannie argued with her on the radio about whether or not she should go. Daniel needed to have a conversation with the man they were chasing first. This would be his only chance to get in there ahead of her.

He stole around to the rear entrance of the building and stayed low as he moved along the corridors. The man was holed up in the hallway leading to the gym. Few doors and no windows.

When Daniel arrived, he adopted a non-threatening posture and stepped around the corner, hands in the air. "Don't shoot."

A big man, six feet away, whirled to face him. A butcher knife in his right hand reflected light from the fluorescent fixture above. "Who are you? Police?"

"I'm not an officer. But they're coming soon. I just want to talk to you." The smell of the man's fear mixed with the distinctive odor of sweating children permeated the hallway by the gymnasium. Daniel kept his hands visible.

"You look like police." His neck corded as his face reddened with renewed anger. "Why should I talk to you? You didn't help when my son was killed, and now you want to put me in jail."

"I'm sorry about your son." Daniel adopted a gentle tone. "I give you my word that I'm not a cop." He drew a deep breath and let it out. "But I do need to know something about your relationship with Tariq Ghazzi. Are you a member of his cell? Did you kill him?" Daniel took a step closer. "Please. We don't have much time. I need to—"

"Who is this Ghazzi? The man looked at him like he was speaking Chinese. "I kill no one." The man slashed the knife through the air. "Not even that devil, Major. But the authorities think I did. And now they will take me to prison." His eyes widened, the sound of running footsteps echoing through the empty halls. "You lied to me."

The knife flashed as the man charged. Daniel twisted his torso like a bullfighter and brought his left hand down on his attacker's right wrist in a practiced maneuver. The ring of metal on concrete sounded as the weapon fell to the floor. In one smooth move, Daniel yanked the big man's left arm behind him and used his own momentum to land him on his back.

Rolling him over, Daniel brought his assailant's hands together and reached behind his own back for—no cuffs. Of course. A pair dangled before his eyes.

BERNIE WATCHED in amazement as Daniel landed Kabir on his back. When it was clear he needed handcuffs, she offered hers. How did he know how to do all that? She alerted the rest of the team and helped Daniel get Kabir to his feet.

"We'll talk later. She glanced at him. "Stick with me."

Breathing hard, Daniel nodded.

"Come on, Mr. Nayar. You've caused enough trouble today."

"Lady Detective. I do not know this Ghazzi. I know nothing about—" The big man glowered at Daniel. "Ow. Watch where you walk. You stepped on my foot."

"You should be quiet until you get to the precinct," Daniel said.

"Okay." The man flinched. "Quit squeezing my arm so tight. I will report you for police brutality."

Daniel rolled his eyes at Bernie as she handed Nayar over to the officers.

"You seem to forget you're a doctor, Doctor—not a lawyer or a police officer." She faced Daniel. "You have no business advising my suspect of his rights."

"I'm—"

She stepped closer. "And what were you doing sneaking into a police operation? You could have been killed."

"May I speak now?"

"Yes." She glared at him.

"I heard the whole thing on the police scanner in autopsy, and when I heard you ask to go in around back, I got worried." He shrugged. "It was stupid, I know, but ... I care about you."

No doubt, he did hear it on the scanner, but she bet that was the only true statement out of his mouth. "What made you think you could protect me better than trained police officers?" And how did he get there ahead of her?

"I didn't think. I reacted."

"Come on. We need to catch up with my prisoner." Her heart

would rather believe he was stupid enough to barrel into the middle of a stand-off than be acting on his own secret agenda, but her head ... Where was a candy machine when she needed it?

The late afternoon sun shone through the school's main lobby doors. Each step amped up the tension in her body. They pushed through the doors shading their eyes against the glare. Police officers hurried toward them. She froze as the big man ahead of her roared. With his hands still handcuffed behind his back, Nayar managed to shake off the men holding him like they were children.

"No." Bernie lunged for him but missed.

He broke to his left, head down like a football player bent on making a touchdown.

21

The crack of a gunshot.

The air around her filled with screams.

Someone tackled her.

"Let me up." She struggled against the body pinning her to the ground.

"Not till it's safe."

Daniel. Relief pulsed through her. Followed by anger and frustration. She pushed against him and sat up. Three feet away, EMTs worked on Kabir Nayar. Blood soaked the ground where he lay. Bernie searched the scene. Jeannie? She sat on the step of an ambulance. Daniel helped Bernie to her feet.

"Don't go anywhere." She stabbed him in the chest with her finger and wove her way over to her friend and partner.

"Is Nayar okay?" Jeannie said.

"I'm not sure. They're working on him now. Where's Mrs. Nayar?"

"I had an officer take her to a neighbor's house while you were inside."

"How are you?" Bernie adjusted the blanket on Jeannie's shoulders.

"I tripped. Opened up my cut." Jeannie raised her freshly bandaged arm. "Where'd lover-boy come from?"

"It's a long story." Bernie turned to watch the forensics people snapping pictures. "Do we have any idea what happened?"

"Yeah." Jeannie cradled her injured forearm in her right hand. "One of our guys got trigger happy." Jeannie stood, letting the blanket drop from her shoulders. "I think it's time I check on our guy." Holding her damaged arm close to her body, she forged a path through the clusters of people to the spot where Kabir Nayar was loaded onto a stretcher.

Daniel had followed directions for once and stood where Bernie had left him. She scanned the scene. Yellow crime tape—and a few imposing men in blue—kept outsiders and press at bay.

A public relations officer spoke to the press on the perimeter. Ms. Belkin was surrounded by a group of women with children. Bernie didn't envy her right now. Where had Ursula Pidgeon gone? There. In that grove of elm trees. She was on her phone. A man stood next to her dressed in dirty blue jeans with an STP patch, a plaid shirt, sleeves rolled up, and a dingy T-shirt. She'd seen him before, but where?

Bernie steered a course in their direction. Ms. Pidgeon angled her body away from Bernie. The man faced her, his hooded eyes dark and unwelcoming.

"Excuse me. I need to speak with Ms. Pidgeon."

"She's on the phone." He positioned himself between Bernie and Pidgeon.

Bernie stiffened and displayed her badge. "She needs to get off the phone."

He tapped Ursula Pidgeon on the shoulder. "Sis, it's that lady detective."

Sis? "You're Ms. Pidgeon's brother?"

"Wow." He placed a grimy hand over his heart. "You really are a good detective."

Too bad there wasn't a law against insulting a police officer. She'd arrest this one in a heartbeat.

"Don't mind my brother." Pidgeon glared at him. "Caleb's had his share of troubles with the law."

The wiry young man snorted.

"But not anymore. Right, Caleb?" She patted his arm. "He's our groundskeeper here at the school." She gestured to the lawns. "And he does a great job."

That's where Bernie had seen him. He'd been coming out of the school that first day—the day she and Jeannie arrived to interview everyone about Ghazzi's murder.

"I was calling all our parents to let them know everything is okay here." Pidgeon flipped a smile at Bernie. "It is, isn't it?" She frowned. "I mean, we can hold school tomorrow as usual?"

Bernie shook her head. "I can't answer that yet. But we'll let you know as soon as possible."

"We have an obligation to our students."

"I realize that, but I'm not the one who makes those decisions."

"Of course." The other woman tempered the tone of her voice. "Sorry. What did you want to ask me?"

"I don't see the teachers around," Bernie said.

"Ms. Belkin released them. She said we know them and where they live, so they shouldn't have to stick around. And the children too."

"Ms. Belkin didn't have the authority to make *that* decision." She bit her lip to control her anger. "We'll need the names of all the students and faculty who were here this afternoon when the shooting took place."

"I'll have that for you as soon as I can get to my computer." Her cell phone rang, and she twitched.

It was a small movement, but Bernie caught it. A boyfriend? Wondering why she'd cut him off earlier? "Thanks. I'll let you get back to your calls." She stuck out her hand to Caleb. "Glad to meet you."

He gripped her hand briefly and mumbled something, but it was long enough. Strong hands, and a tattoo of STP on the inside of his wrist. She'd keep her eye on this one.

As she steered a path toward Ms. Belkin, Jeannie grabbed her arm.

"Santos, I'm going to speak to Mrs. Nayar. Now comes the hard part. It's not like I haven't done this a million times. But for some reason, this woman gets to me."

"I can talk to her." Maybe she and Jeannie were more alike than Bernie thought. She climbed into the car next to Jeannie.

"Can you open this?" Jeannie picked up her water bottle.

Bernie twisted the cap. "Where's Daniel?"

"Rose needed him back at the morgue." Jeannie took a swig. "I'll take care of Mrs. Nayar. Would you talk to Belkin and get that list of teachers and students?"

"Will do. See you later." Bernie stepped back as the police car surged forward. She found the head of the school slumped on a bench, her head in her hands. "Ms. Belkin? I have a few questions. Mind if I sit?"

The older woman straightened and slid over to make room for Bernie. "Why did you let your teachers and students leave the scene without permission?"

"Ms. Pidgeon said she spoke to your partner, Detective Jansen, and that she suggested I reduce the number of people crowding the scene. I did so immediately."

"When was this?" Bernie retrieved her phone from her pocket and made a note to check with Jeannie.

"Right before you appeared with poor Mr. Nayar. Is he going to be okay?"

"Too soon to tell. How well do you know the Nayars?"

"Not that well. Their son went to our school—before his death."

"We understand he was killed on a school outing?" Bernie said.

Ms. Belkin nodded. "There was an unfortunate bus accident, and five children were killed."

"Did the parents hold the school responsible?"

"Yes." She sighed. "After the criminal case was thrown out, the parents brought a civil suit against the school." Ms. Belkin clenched her hands in her lap. "It was recently ruled in favor of the school."

"Do you think that's why Kabir Nayar sent all those hate emails to Mr. Major?"

She looked up. "I didn't know about any emails."

"Are you from around here, Ms. Belkin?" Bernie studied the woman.

Her eyes widened. "No. I grew up in Indianapolis. Why do you ask?"

"Just wondered if you knew Mr. Majors before he came to St. Martins. Did you?"

She turned her head. A cloud passed over the sun, making it hard for Bernie to tell if there was a shadow or a blush on the woman's face. What was she thinking about?

"No, Detective, not before." A slight smile lifted the corners of her lips. "He could be a charmer when he wanted to be. We had a brief fling. He said he had Sicilian ancestry on his mother's side." She sighed. "I suppose I wanted to believe him." She cleared her throat. "I always thought that explained that touch of cruelty he exhibited. I was a fool."

"It can happen to any of us, Ms. Belkin." Bernie closed notes on her phone. "Believe me."

<hr/>

THE LIGHTS in the autopsy room seemed especially bright today as Daniel handed his aunt an instrument she needed. They worked well together, and he enjoyed her banter. But today was different.

While Daniel's body performed the autopsies with his aunt,

his mind remained at St. Martin's Preparatory School. The sound of the gunshot transported Daniel back in time. As the man fell, he saw his partner fall. Not again. He wouldn't lose another woman he cared for—he couldn't survive it. He'd thrown Bernie to the ground and covered her body with his. Which only made her madder than before.

Bernie saw him take Nayar down, and he was tired of thinking up lies to explain his actions. She didn't buy them anyway. Time to tell her the truth. He texted her an invitation to get together that evening.

As he finished the paperwork on his aunt's latest patient, his phone chirped. Bernie agreed to see him later at her house. He felt better than he had for a long time.

"That's it for today, Danny." Rose walked to the sink. "How about supper with your dear old aunt?"

"Not tonight, okay?" He patted her back.

"If you want to check on your lady detective, just say so." She winked at him.

"You could always see right through me." He laughed. "See you tomorrow."

<hr>

BERNIE LAID her phone on her desk and stared at the window across the room. Why would Daniel want to get together? He had to realize that she'd have lots of questions for him about today. Why wasn't he avoiding her? He must have concocted his story already. She shook her head. Not this time, Danny boy. Tonight, she would learn the truth.

"Detective Santos?" A policewoman appeared next to Bernie's desk.

She started. "Yes."

"Henry Abbott's attorney is here. He wants to speak to whoever's in charge of his murder investigation." She held out a business card.

"I'll take care of it." Bernie stood and put on her jacket. "Thanks." She walked to reception, where a gentleman in a three-piece gray suit sat. "I'm Detective Santos. How can I help you?"

"Oscar Covington." He rose, grabbing his briefcase beside him, and stuck out his hand. "I represent the estate of Henry Abbott. Is there somewhere we can speak in private?"

"Sure." Bernie swiped her ID at the door, and they made their way back to her desk. "Will this do?'

He looked around the almost empty room. "Yes." He eyed Bernie. "According to the papers, Mr. Abbott's death has been declared a homicide."

"Yes, we're treating it as a murder by person or persons unknown at this time."

"In the event Mr. Abbott was murdered, he entrusted me with this letter for the detectives who would be investigating his case." He opened his briefcase, withdrew a manila envelope and held it close to his chest. "You are the detective on his case, aren't you?"

"Yes, Mr. Covington, along with Detective Jeannie Jansen."

"This is a first for me." He handed her the envelope and a paper to sign stating she had received the letter. "I hope it helps catch his killer."

"Me too." She rose and shook hands once again with the attorney. "This officer will see you out." She motioned to a policeman near the door. "Thank you for coming."

A letter from a dead man, which contained information that might solve one—possibly two—murders. Bernie's fingertips itched to undo the clasp. She should wait for her partner. She stared at the manila envelope a minute longer before picking up her phone and punching in Jeannie's number.

22

Bernie sighed and placed the unopened envelope on Jeannie's desk. She picked up the Nayars' file that Bulldog had brought this morning. So sad about their son. A newspaper article told the story of the terrible accident, the unsuccessful criminal case, and the civil case settled in favor of the school. That must have been what Mrs. Nayar meant when she said the devil took Kabir's heart and hers as well.

Losing the civil case must have been the last straw. Mr. Nayar sent hate emails to Mr. Majors/Tariq Ghazzi, and when that wasn't enough to satisfy his need for justice, he killed him. Now she could lose her husband too. Bernie flipped through some pages. No family listed for either Nayar. But she did discover one interesting fact.

Jeannie barreled into the room and made a beeline for her desk. "Sorry to take so long. Where's this letter?" She worked her hands into gloves and undid the envelope's clasp.

Bernie did the same. Despite Jeannie's usual impatience, when it came to evidence, she knew how to do her job. She withdrew the contents and began to read. She finished a page and handed it to Bernie.

After two pages, a low whistle sounded from Jeannie. "No wonder Ghazzi was willing to pay Abbott every month."

"You do realize we need to bring in the FBI?" Bernie said. "This is way over our paygrade."

"Yeah, but not right away. Let's see if we can't solve our murders first." Jeannie gathered the papers together and slid them into the envelope. "Where do you think he got this?"

"Didn't he have a sister who was involved with Ghazzi in Cleveland?" Bernie stripped off her gloves and threw them in the trashcan.

"Yeah, but why would she give this to her brother who despised him?"

"Maybe she didn't. Maybe he found it after she died."

Jeannie drummed her fingers on the desk. "I wish he'd written a letter of explanation with this stuff. Or at least something to point us to who might have killed for it."

"Besides Ghazzi—who was already dead." Bernie paused. "How was your talk with Mrs. Nayar?" Bernie spoke in a soft voice.

"Okay. She's at the hospital waiting for Kabir to wake up. The docs said it's touch and go with him. He's lost a lot of blood." She frowned. "She did tell me she remembered something else about the white truck." Jeannie waved her hand in the air. "Anyway. The truck was big and had a dent over the right rear wheel well."

"Not much more help, but it narrows the field some. I'll tell Bulldog to take out all the light-duty pickups." Bernie stretched. "I'm meeting Daniel tonight. Maybe we'll find out what's really going on with him."

"We could get one mystery solved at least."

<hr />

THE DELICIOUS SMELL of burgers and onions preceded Daniel into Bernie's house. "I come bearing gifts." He held out the bag of burgers and fries from Little Joe's Sandwich Shop. "Where should I—"

Wolf whistle. "Hello, handsome."

What was that?

"Lori. Hush." Bernie appeared from the kitchen with a green parrot on her shoulder. "Sorry. I rescued her from a crime scene, and her previous owner taught her some bad habits." She crossed the room to a large cage situated on the other side of the room. "In you go, missy."

"Wait." Daniel set the food on the counter. "Does she bite? May I hold her?"

"Lori Darling has never bitten anyone." Bernie grinned. "That I know of. Put your hand against her chest. She'll step onto your fingers."

The emerald green bird climbed onto Daniel's hand and up his arm. She nibbled on his hair.

"Lori, don't." Bernie moved to retrieve her bird.

Daniel stroked the soft feathers. " It's okay. I don't mind."

The parrot pressed her beak to his cheek. "Give us a kiss."

"Gee, Lori, we just met." Daniel chuckled.

"She likes you." Bernie gave him a soft smile.

"But what does your owner think of me?" Daniel twisted his head as if talking to Lori. "That's the real question."

Bernie stiffened. "I'm hungry. Let's get you back in your cage so we can eat." She took the bird on her arm and placed her in the cage.

"See you later, handsome." Squawk.

"We'll eat over there." Bernie pointed to her left.

Daniel scanned the tidy room with its colorful walls and comfortable furniture. A table sat in one corner with two chairs.

"Iced tea, pop, or water?"

"Water's good."

She returned with two placemats, two waters, paper plates, and napkins. "Thanks for this. I haven't eaten all day."

Small talk and food filled the next fifteen minutes while he gathered his courage. Telling Bernie the truth about his real job and why he was here would mean disobeying a direct order from his superior. He could get fired. But somehow, he knew in his gut that it was the right thing to do. He wiped his mouth and took a deep breath.

"I'm an undercover agent for the FBI."

Bernie eyed him. "No offense, but do you have any ID?"

"I would have been disappointed in you if you hadn't asked." He laid his open credentials in front of her.

"Thank you." She scooted her chair back, went over to him, and gave him a kiss on the cheek. After regaining her seat, she gave him a broad smile. "That makes more sense than the scenario Jeannie and I came up with."

"What did you two think?"

"At one point, we wondered if you might be an industrial spy for the mining industry."

"Where did that come from?"

"The rock used to kill Ghazzi came from a mine." She gestured with a French fry. "At that time, we thought you might be involved somehow."

Daniel threw his head back in laughter.

"So, what did bring you to Pleasant Valley?"

"Tariq Ghazzi—but not to kill him. I was supposed to find him and bring him back to Cleveland. He was an HVE, Homegrown Violent Extremist. Several years ago, we learned he was planning an attack on a synagogue in Cleveland in the name of ISIS.

"Everything went sideways when one of our raids went terribly wrong. The place was booby-trapped, and everyone was killed—at least we thought everybody died. It seemed Ghazzi escaped, and valuable information went missing."

"I may be able to help with that," Bernie said. "But go on."

Daniel cocked an eyebrow at her. "What do you mean?"

"I shouldn't have said anything." She grimaced. "It's police business. Finish your story. I promise to tell you more as soon as I can."

"Hmm. I'll hold you to that promise." He captured her eyes with his for a brief moment. "Anyway, we received a tip that Tariq was living down here near where he grew up."

"We found a photo at Henry Abbott's place of him, Abbott, and their sisters."

Maybe she and Jeannie found more than just a picture in their search.

He nodded. "He and his step-sister and step-brother lived on a farm not too far from here. I am a doctor, by the way. So, I was chosen for this assignment because I could have a credible cover story."

"Are his brother and sister still in the area?"

"As far as we know. His brother's a bad one, taking after their parents. We think he may be responsible for making explosives for different criminal elements—including possible terrorists. Their mom and dad were members of a 1960s-70s counterculture group called Serenity, Tranquility, and Peace.

"They moved here from Colorado after things got too hot for them there. But they never stopped living a life of drugs, thievery, and violence. I heard the sister managed to break away from that lifestyle." Daniel cleared his throat. "I have another confession to make."

◦────────────────◦

THE ATMOSPHERE CHANGED. A chill ran down her spine.

"Something else happened during that raid in Cleveland that I think you should know about."

She couldn't swallow. She wanted to cover her ears, change the subject, or tell him it didn't matter. But it did matter, and she did need to hear what he was about to say.

"I killed my partner that night." His eyes held hers. "It was a close-quarters gunfight, and she jumped into my crossfire at the last moment. It's taken me a year to even touch a gun again. This has been my first real field assignment since the incident—that's what they call it. I call it the nightmare."

What words of comfort or wisdom could she, a brand-new detective, possibly offer? Tears flowed down her cheeks.

"Daniel, I—" She took his hand and pulled him into an embrace. It was all she had to give. Her shoulder grew damp with his weeping.

After several moments, his lips found hers in a soft kiss. He stroked her cheek with his thumb.

"I've lived with—" His phone sprang to life on the table. A picture of his aunt came on the screen. "I better take this."

Fear gripped Bernie's heart as the color drained from Daniel's face

23

D aniel's blood froze as a male voice sounded in his ear. "If you want your aunt to live, leave Pleasant Valley tonight."

"Why are you doing this? I'm a doctor—"

"We know who you really are and why you're here. You can't fool us."

"I'm not trying to fool anyone." Daniel ran a hand through his hair.

"You assassinated Ghazzi, and now your cell wants to take over our territory." A loud noise like wood slamming on wood sounded close. "We won't let that happen. Go home to Cleveland." The phone went dead.

Daniel clenched his fists as an arrow of regret shot through his chest. "They've kidnapped Aunt Rose, and it's all my fault."

"Do you want to call in your FBI resources?" Bernie placed a hand on his arm.

"No. They took her, so I'd leave town." Daniel glowered. "My cover is too good. They think I'm a member of the cell in Cleveland—the one Ghazzi belonged to."

"Why is that such a problem?"

"Territories. This is theirs. They think I killed Ghazzi out of revenge, and now my gang wants to start a takeover."

Bernie paced. "What are you really working on now that Ghazzi is dead?"

"Who killed him. That's why I was at the school this afternoon. I wanted to talk to Nayar before you got to him." He tried to focus on Bernie's questions, but he couldn't think straight. "I was sure he was hired by a local cell to kill Ghazzi."

"Did you talk to him?"

"That's what's so strange. He didn't recognize the name."

"What name?"

"Ghazzi." Daniel rubbed the back of his neck. "He denies killing anybody. And I believe him." He looked at his phone. "But that doesn't help Aunt Rose. I'm going to her house."

"I'm going with you, and I'm calling Jeannie to meet us."

"No." Daniel rounded on her. "No police. He'll kill her. I need to do this alone."

"Come on, Daniel, you're FBI. You know how this goes. Besides, the police are already involved." She pointed to herself. "You can trust me. And you can trust Jeannie. I won't tell her why she's meeting us until she's there, and we have a chance to talk." Bernie stuck her gun in her holster. "I'm coming."

Anger, fear, and resignation raced through him in rapid succession. "Let's go."

They sped toward his aunt's home, and the lights of the small-town streets soon faded into the dark of country roads. As they pulled into the isolated drive of Rose O'Leary's cottage, lamps glowed in every window, and classical music floated through the air. The splintered wood around the lock on the front door offered the only evidence that anything was wrong. Bernie and Daniel drew their guns and approached.

"Aunt Rose?" Daniel said. "Bernie and I came to visit for a minute. Are you home?"

No answer. His stomach clenched.

A car roared up behind Daniel's. "What's going on here?" Jeannie slammed her door.

Bernie motioned her over. "Rose has been kidnapped. Don't call it in yet. Let's get inside first. I'll explain in a minute."

"Rose?" Daniel stepped around the threshold into the living room. A chair lay on its side by the fireplace, and a lamp was smashed by his feet. He stayed to the perimeter of the room and moved down the hall to the two small bedrooms and the kitchen. "She's not here." He holstered his weapon. He should have left town. If she died—

"Unless you two can give me a really good reason, I'm calling out the big guns," Jeannie said.

"Wait." Daniel held up a hand. "I need to tell you something."

After letting Jeannie in on everything, Bernie and Daniel convinced her to hold off long enough for the three of them to take a look around. Donning booties and gloves Jeannie had in her car, each took a section of the house and agreed to search without moving anything.

"Does your aunt paint her nails?" Bernie squatted near an overturned chair in the living room.

"No way. With all the solvents she uses at work, she keeps them short and unpolished." Daniel wove his way through the room to see what she was looking at. Jeannie joined them.

"Does that look like hot pink to you?" Bernie took a pen and lifted the false fingernail while shining her light on it.

"Yes." Jeannie nodded. "And we both know someone who uses that color."

"Ursula Pidgeon," Bernie said.

"Who's that?" Daniel said.

"We'll brief you on the way." Jeannie headed toward the front door. "Now I call forensics. And we pay a visit to Ms. Pidgeon."

THE CAR CAREENED AROUND A CURVE, and Bernie struggled to click her seatbelt. "Slow down, Jeannie, or we'll be dead before we can save Rose."

Her partner didn't answer but eased the pressure on the accelerator. Bernie breathed relief and glanced over her shoulder at Daniel, his grim expression revealed briefly in the oncoming headlights.

"Do you have a photo of this Ursula Pidgeon?"

Bernie twisted in her seat to face him, scrolled to a photo, and handed it to Daniel.

He frowned. "I saw her with you and another woman on the lawn of the school earlier today." He returned her phone. "You think she's involved in Aunt Rose's kidnapping?"

"She wears hot pink false nails." Bernie grabbed the handle above the door as Jeannie made a sharp right turn.

"There's the house." Jeannie pulled to the curb and cut the engine.

"Shouldn't we wait for back-up?"

"It might be too late by then." Daniel was out of the car and headed for the house.

Bernie hurried after them, assured this was a bad idea. On the porch, the three paused, guns drawn, and made eye contact before Bernie banged on the door.

"Police. Open up." Lights shone through the lightweight curtains covering the windows. She knocked harder. "Open the door, Ms. Pidgeon. Police."

No sound of movement from within. Bernie nodded to Daniel, who slammed his foot against the flimsy wood door. One more kick and the door burst open. Bernie crouched and slid inside to the left. Daniel followed, and Jeannie entered last, closing the door behind her. With practiced efficiency, the three law enforcement officers split up and searched Ursula Pidgeon's home.

"Clear." Daniel joined Bernie and Jeannie in the living room. "Have you found anything?"

"Could Pidgeon and her brother be Ghazzi's step-sister and step-brother?" Jeannie held up photos from a shoebox. "Look at these."

"That's why she looked so familiar." Daniel reached for the photographs. The picture of a boy and a girl in their mid to late teens and a toddler standing in front of a barn fluttered to the floor.

Bernie picked it up. "Is this their farm?"

He studied the photo again. "It could be—probably is. I'm not sure where it's located, but I have an idea."

"Doesn't matter. I've got Bulldog." Jeannie yanked out her phone.

24

"According to Bulldog's instructions, we turn right here." Bernie peered into the gathering darkness. She knew this area. They passed the entrance to Nate and Madison Zuberi's subdivision and Lake Pleasant a few miles back. A gravel path not much wider than the car appeared between two fence posts.

"How much farther to the farmhouse?" Jeannie steered the automobile off the pavement. The headlights shone along a weedy drive that disappeared over a hill.

Bernie squinted at her phone. "Half a mile."

"Best if we leave the car here and walk the rest of the way." Jeannie swung the car off the rocks and into the vegetation along the side. "Backup is still ten minutes out. Rose could be dead by then." She checked her weapon and pushed her door open.

Daniel did the same.

"At least take the time to put on a vest." Bernie grabbed him by the arm, ran to the trunk, and threw one to him and then Jeannie. After putting on hers, she examined her gun.

"You don't have one that says FBI on it, do you?" Daniel tapped his chest protection.

"Why? You think these bad guys only shoot at police?" Jeannie snorted.

"A man can hope."

Bernie gave a little laugh, glad for the brief release of tension. She'd been in takedowns before but always with support. She wiped her hands on her pants. *Lord, keep us safe.*

The trio stopped at the end of the drive. A weak dusk-to-dawn light illuminated a dirt yard with an old white farmhouse and a ramshackle barn. It was evident no one had lived here for a long time, and if it weren't for the lights on in the buildings and the two vehicles parked in the yard, Bernie wouldn't have believed anyone was there now.

"Not a good idea for us to split up. We need to stay together." Daniel peered up the road.

"I agree." Bernie followed his gaze.

"Probably so. The barn first and then the house." Jeannie moved from shadow to shadow, and the other two followed. Near the barn, they heard someone humming softly. Jeannie motioned she'd investigate and crept around the corner.

Bernie fought to remain still in the tall grass. At last, her partner tapped on her shoulder. The two women edged over to where Daniel remained hidden.

"I only see one man," Jeannie whispered loud enough for them to hear. "He's working on something. No hostage in sight."

"Why don't you come in from the other side while Daniel and I enter from the front," Bernie said. "We'll get him under control and move to the house. Okay?"

Crouching low, Jeannie crossed in front of the barn and prepared to turn the corner. Her foot caught on something, and the distinctive clang of metal on metal rang out in the still night. She held her position.

The man stopped humming. Bernie held her breath. Daniel stiffened beside her. When the man's tuneless song began again, Bernie felt her lungs expand. She glanced at Jeannie and nodded.

The barn door exploded open, and a screech filled the air. Light poured out, catching Jeannie like a deer in headlights.

"I'm not going to jail." The man stood on the threshold, holding a shotgun.

"Police." Bernie ran from the shadows. "Put the gun down, or I'll shoot." She lifted her arm, aiming as she went.

The screen door to the house slammed back on its hinges, and a woman burst through.

Ursula Pidgeon leaped from the porch. "Caleb, no."

The man swiveled and fired.

All the air was sucked from the farmyard. Ursula's painful scream acted as a call to action. Jeannie raced to the stricken woman.

"Mama." Caleb threw his gun on the ground. He took a step toward Ursula, hesitated, and sprinted across the yard toward his pickup.

Bernie chased after him, but he beat her to it. Gunning the engine, he aimed the big truck right at her and Daniel. Her shots ricocheted off the solid metal careening her way. She dove to her right and covered her face with her hands to keep from choking in the dust cloud.

When she opened her eyes, Daniel's slack features sliced her heart in two. Blood dripped from his nose.

"Dear God, no." She touched his cheek with shaking fingers.

He moaned.

"Daniel. Thank God. You're alive." She helped him to his feet.

"Maybe a cracked rib or two." He dabbed his nose and winced. "But nothing major. Fender caught me on the way down."

Tires sprayed dirt and gravel as the white truck escaped down the road.

"Where's that backup?" Jeannie cursed.

"We need an ambulance." Bernie's concerned gaze shifted between Daniel and Ursula Pidgeon.

"Already called for one." Jeannie turned toward the house. "I need to look for Rose."

Bernie's throat constricted. "I'll go."

Sirens wailed louder, and the familiar cars poured into the area. She headed for the farmhouse and the hunt for Rose. Bounding up the wooden porch stairs, she wrenched the door open, and Rose collapsed into her arms.

"I need help here."

Daniel appeared by her side, and they managed to drag Rose to a bench nearby. He slid next to his aunt.

"Rose, am I glad to see you." Bernie squatted in front of the M.E. and looked into her eyes.

"I'm glad you see me too, child." She gave the detective a weak smile.

<hr>

DANIEL O'LEARY ENTERED the emergency room for the second time in less than a week. After getting his ribs checked out, he looked in on his Aunt Rose.

"Bruised, not broken," he said. "I wish it were me lying there instead of you."

"Don't be silly." She scowled. "I'm fine. A little check, and they'll be sending me home."

"Sure. And I'll grow wings and fly." Daniel flapped his hands like a bird, then grimaced.

"You've always been the crazy one in the family, Daniel, my boy. But it would be good to have you stay for a time." She winked. "Just until my wings are stronger."

He shook his head. "You're determined to get me under your watchful eye, aren't you?"

"After what's been happening, I think it might be a very good idea for us to band together."

"You may be right about that, Aunt Rose." He sighed. *No more lies.* That would be nice. Although, she may not want anything to do with him after she learned the truth. He pulled a chair closer to the bed. "I have something to tell you."

When he finished, she lay so still. Had she fallen asleep? He hoped not. He didn't think he could go through this again.

"Aunt Rose? Did you hear me?"

"I heard you, Daniel." A tear slid down her familiar face and burned a hole in his heart. "I love you more than any son I could have had of my own. You can tell me anything. You could have trusted me. I would have kept your secret."

"It is—*was*—my job." Daniel closed his eyes. "I swore never to break my cover with anyone."

She swiveled her head to face him. "What happens now? Will you be fired?"

"I don't know." He rubbed his neck. "Maybe." Or worse.

25

"Do they think Ursula Pidgeon will make it?" Bernie leaned against the wall in the hospital waiting room.

"She took a blast to the stomach." Jeannie paced back and forth. "She's in surgery now. The doctor says the next twenty-four hours are critical."

Bernie fingered the medallion in her pocket. *Lord, please heal her.*

Jeannie stopped in front of her. "What's going on in the search for Caleb?"

"I put out an all-points bulletin on him and his truck. Person of Interest." She glanced at her phone. "Now it's a waiting game until someone spots him. He tried to run me down. I hope—"

"Bernie, don't let your personal feelings take over." Jeannie's tone softened. "I know from experience."

"I'm not."

"Yeah, you are. I see it in your eyes." Jeannie pointed to Bernie's cell phone. "And you're about to crush your phone. This won't be the last time a perp tries to kill you."

"You get mad about things. How do you justify your anger?" Was she overstepping her bounds?

"Yeah," Jeannie said. "I got a quick temper, and I know it.

But I'm working on it. I try to remind myself that the bad guy is trying to get away, and he doesn't care how he does it. He doesn't want to go to prison. He's acting on instinct. For him, it's nothing personal. I just happen to be in the way." Jeannie sighed. "Besides, if you really needed to stop him, you'd shoot him. Right? It wouldn't be personal for you. Just doing what you needed to do to serve and protect."

Could she have shot Caleb? "I hope it never comes to that."

"So do I, for your sake as much as for the other guy."

The doctor rounded the corner and headed straight for them. "I'm afraid I have some bad news."

Bernie and Jeannie shared a sidelong glance.

"Ms. Pidgeon came through the surgery, but she's in a deep coma. We have no idea when or if she'll ever recover."

"I guess seeing her is out of the question?" Jeannie said.

The doctor waved a hand in the air. "You can see her, but it won't do any good. She's not responding to anyone or anything. Leave your number at the nurse's desk in case things change." He walked away.

"Come on, Jeannie. He's right." Bernie tugged on her partner's arm. "We have other leads to follow."

"Like what? Until we find Caleb, what—" She yanked her ringing phone from her purse. "Jansen." Jeannie listened, then pushed end. "We're needed back at the station."

"They found him?" Bernie quickened her pace to keep up with her partner.

"No, but some woman is waiting for us back at the precinct. She claims to have information about our case."

"Did they give you any idea who she is?" Bernie pushed through the doors of the hospital to the parking lot.

"Not a clue."

"I guess we'll find out soon enough."

As THEY ENTERED THE PRECINCT, Bernie spied the sable-haired woman slouched in Jeannie's chair. She'd propped her boots on her partner's desk. Not a smart idea.

"Easy." Bernie grabbed Jeannie's arm. "We need to hear what she has to say before you chew her up and spit her out."

Jeannie took a deep breath. "Right." She sauntered over to her desk, smiled, and patted the chair next to her. "Guests usually sit on this side."

"Sorry." The woman lifted her feet and let them down without a sound. "I try to catch a few minutes of sleep when I can. Didn't mean to offend." She rose and slipped around the desk to the proffered chair. "I'm Zoe Poole." She offered her hand across the desk. "I work for RPI."

"Isn't that Rafe's private investigative firm?" Bernie pulled up a chair nearby. "Do you know Madison Long Zuberi?"

"Yes, and yes. She's away on her honeymoon, isn't she?"

"She is," Bernie said. "What brings you here?"

"I think it's time we join forces." Zoe leaned forward. "I've been hired to investigate the murder of Philip Major—Tariq Ghazzi."

"By whom?" Bernie rolled her chair over to her desk to grab her phone and rolled back.

"By the insurance company." She glanced between the detectives. "Ursula Pidgeon and Tariq Ghazzi were not brother and sister. Well, they were. But he was adopted."

Bernie paused in her notes. She had a feeling about what was coming next.

"They were lovers too. And Caleb is not Ursula's brother. He's her son. Hers and Ghazzi's."

Of course. That explained why Caleb called Ursula mama after he shot her.

Jeannie tapped the desk with her finger. "What am I missing here?"

"Ghazzi left a substantial insurance policy. Ursula's already filed a claim. But if she killed him, then, of course, she can't inherit. Same with Caleb. Do you believe either Ursula or Caleb murdered Tariq Ghazzi?"

"What do you think?" Jeannie glared at her.

Zoe shook her head. "What evidence I've seen doesn't support that."

"What evidence?"

"The rock for one thing." Zoe waved her hand. "I can't see either of them hitting him over the head. Stabbing makes more sense for those two." She pursed her lips. "And why go to all the trouble of spreading sulfur on the hearth?"

"How did you get access to the rock and the crime scene description?" Jeannie's hands curled into fists.

"Rafe has an agreement with your captain."

"He would." Jeannie pressed her lips together. "Our captain is your co-worker's husband."

Zoe looked at Bernie.

"Jeannie gets territorial where crime scene evidence is concerned." Bernie flipped through her notes. "Caleb and his sis —mother kidnapped Rose O'Leary and shot at Daniel O'Leary. Will that keep them from inheriting?"

"That must have to do with their business. Which I know nothing about." Zoe turned her chair toward Bernie. "They can inherit if convicted of any crime other than killing Tariq Ghazzi."

"Even if either of them killed Henry Abbott?" Bernie said. "What do you think? Were either of them involved?"

"I have my suspicions." Zoe lifted her chin.

"Which are?" Bernie said. "You do realize that withholding any evidence is obstruction of justice?"

She nodded. "I know. But right now, it's only supposition. I believe Caleb was involved in Abbott's murder somehow."

"Why didn't you come forward sooner?" Bernie glanced at Jeannie when she heard the snap of a pencil breaking.

"Hang on," Zoe said. "I said pretty sure. If you want concrete evidence, I'll be glad to help. That's why I'm here." She folded her arms across her chest. "But don't go all Rambo on me, Detective, or I'll walk out that door."

"We all want the same thing." Bernie eyed Jeannie. "To catch the killers. Please." A giggle threatened to escape as Bernie surveyed Zoe in her green camo outfit, complete with combat boots. She's calling Jeannie Rambo? "I'm getting a coffee. Anyone else?"

"Yeah." Jeannie rolled her chair away from her desk.

"Do you have sparkling water?" Zoe said.

Bernie sped from the room, holding her sides in silent laughter. Sparkling water for Rambo it is.

A coffee in each hand and a water bottle in her jacket pocket, Bernie returned to find Jeannie staring at her computer and Zoe with her eyes closed, legs propped on a nearby chair. Bernie envied her ability to nap like that.

"Wake up." She tapped the bottle against Zoe's shoe.

She righted herself, violet eyes clear and bright. "Thanks."

"If Ursula didn't kill Ghazzi, and Caleb didn't kill Ghazzi, who did?" Bernie handed Jeannie her coffee.

"I'm not convinced either of them didn't." Jeannie tapped on her keyboard.

"You may be right," Zoe said. "What were they into?"

Jeannie squinted at the screen.

"Here." Bernie pushed a pair of glasses across the desk.

"Looks like Caleb has had some drug arrests but no convictions." Jeannie grunted. "Wonder why?"

Drugs. No convictions explained how he got work at a school. Could Caleb be a dealer? "Do you think Ursula was involved?"

"Doesn't matter. A mom will do 'most anything to protect her kid. And if something happens to him, look out."

That was so true. Bernie had seen moms run into burning buildings to rescue their children.

"What about Henry Abbott?" Jeannie pulled up another

screen on her computer. "He has another sister, Elsa. Have we ever spoken to her?"

"We haven't been able to find her." Bernie thumbed through her notes.

"I know where she is," Zoe said.

Both detectives stared at the statuesque woman in camo. "Where?" Two voices echoed through the room.

"Why don't I show you?"

"I'm not going anywhere else tonight." Jeannie held her hand up. "Come back tomorrow morning, Ms. Poole."

"I'll call Daniel and let him know where to meet us." Bernie yawned. "He'll want to be in on this. Goodnight, ladies."

◁────────────▷

BERNIE'S MORNING coffee sloshed in her stomach as their Dodge Charger bumped along the country driveway. Elsa's hundred acres abutted Ursula and Caleb's property. Elsa lived in the old farmhouse, a truly isolated existence. Jeannie seemed to hit every hole and rock along the way. In fact, Bernie was sure she aimed for a few of them on purpose.

If it weren't for the obvious tire tracks, she would have thought they were on the wrong road. But a vehicle had passed this way not too long ago. One that dripped oil. If it traveled this road often, it was no surprise.

Unattended orchards filled with scraggly peach trees lined both sides of the road, and the sweet smell of overripe fruit filtered in through the vents. The lane made a sharp left-hand turn, and Jeannie slowed the car to a stop.

A small farmhouse lay ahead, once white, now weathered to gray. The covered porch put the front door and windows into deep shadow. Sunlight sparkled off the surface of a large pond nearby. Parked in the yard was a white truck with a dented right fender.

"I'm calling for backup." Jeannie talked into her phone.

Zoe raised her eyebrows.

"Caleb is here." Bernie pulled her gun from its holster.

Zoe removed a revolver from her camo vest. She flipped open the cylinder, spun it once, and clicked it into place. "Ready."

A soft rap on Bernie's window had both women aiming their guns into Daniel's face through the glass.

"Don't scare me like that." She unlocked the doors. "Get in the back with Zoe."

"I'm Daniel. FBI." Daniel stuck out his hand.

Zoe nodded.

"Do you think he knows we're—"

A shotgun blast shattered the air. With a huge sigh, the car listed to the left.

"He shot out our left tire, the jerk." Jeannie stuck her badge out the driver's side window. "This is police property. You just committed a crime. Come out with your hands up."

"I didn't kill Tariq." Caleb shouted. "Neither did my—neither did Ursula." He cocked the shotgun. "Walk out of here and leave us alone."

Bernie stepped out of the car.

"What are you doing? Are you nuts?" Jeannie made a grab for Bernie's arm but missed.

"Caleb, we're not going away until we've had a chance to talk to Elsa." She stepped forward. "That's what we came for." Could they stall him long enough for backup to get here?

"She's not here."

A chill ran through her. Bernie put a hand on her gun. "Did you kill her?"

"No. I'd never hurt Elsa." His voice echoed off the building. "I love her."

"Where is she?" Bernie shuffled a little closer.

"Work."

"We'll need to see for ourselves." Bernie tried to get a fix on his voice. "You understand."

"You don't believe me. Surprise, surprise." He cackled. "Well, sorry. You'll just have to come back another time."

"Where does she work?"

"You're the detective. Figure it out for yourself."

"Maybe you can help us, Caleb." She shaded her eyes. "Did you know her brother Henry?"

"What about him? He was cruel—especially to Elsa. He got what he deserved."

"When was the last time you spoke to Henry?" Where was he? If only she could see into the shadows. Was that a shotgun next to the door? "Caleb?"

The engine in the white pickup growled alive. Caleb spun the truck around in the dirt, producing a cloud of dust that shrouded the entire area.

Bernie sprang onto the police car. He was not getting another chance to run her down. But would he get away again?

A shot rang out. The truck veered into the police car, pitching Bernie forward over its hood. She slid to the ground and landed on her feet. The driver's door of the pickup slammed open, pinning her between it and the fender. Caleb exited the truck holding his left arm and raced toward the house.

She reached for her gun. Gone. Where was it? She swiveled, scanning the ground.

"Take mine." Zoe handed her revolver to Bernie.

Bernie ran up the steps and into the house. Voices. She listened.

"I don't want to hurt you, but I will." Caleb's words echoed with desperation.

"I can't let you leave," Jeannie said.

As she crept forward, Bernie's heart rate ratcheted upward. In the back yard, Caleb sat astride a four-wheeler. He pointed a gun at Jeannie's chest. She blocked his way, her weapon aimed at him. Bernie stepped onto the back porch.

"Give it up, Caleb." She raised the revolver. Movement to her right.

Daniel approached from Caleb's back. He caught the motion out of the corner of his eye. Hunched over the handlebars, he gunned the machine forward. Straight at Jeannie.

"Jeannie, get out of the way." Bernie's heart leaped into her throat as she watched her partner stand her ground.

At the last second, Caleb steered the four-wheeler past her, reaching out with his left arm and knocking her down as he went by.

Bernie aimed at his retreating back but pulled up when he disappeared around a large tree.

"Can you walk?" Bernie slipped an arm around Jeannie.

"Yeah, just need a couple of aspirin." Jeannie slung her arm around Daniel on the other side. "Now, we can arrest Caleb for assaulting an officer."

"I think he may have done much more than that. You heard him. Henry Abbott was cruel, and he deserved what he got." Bernie supported her. "I believe he killed Abbott out of love for Elsa."

26

"Forensics is in there now." Bernie scanned the faded white boards of the farmhouse. "Let's take a walk-through. If you're up for it."

"I'm fine." Jeannie flexed her shoulder. "Just a few bumps and bruises."

The screen door squeaked, flashing Bernie back to childhood visits to her grandma. A covered sofa and chair, plain wooden table with four chairs, and a television filled the dim interior of the front room. Doorways led to two bedrooms and a bathroom. A central hallway ended in a small kitchen with a back entrance onto another covered porch in the rear.

An antique silver hairbrush, a bottle of inexpensive cologne, and a lipstick lay on the dresser of the largest bedroom. Bernie searched for anything connecting Caleb to Henry Abbott. Under the bed, she found a scrapbook. She needed more time to examine it thoroughly.

Photos in tarnished silver frames showed Caleb Pidgeon. Elsa Abbott must be quite a bit older than Caleb. Were they lovers? The Abbotts and Pidgeons were entangled in many different ways. Did one of those tangles lead to the murder of not one man, but two?

"Bernie," Jeannie's voice sounded from the doorway. "The judge didn't see sufficient evidence to grant a search warrant since the house doesn't belong to Caleb." She gestured toward the album. "Put that back and join me outside."

She laid it on the bed and thumbed open the cover for a quick look before leaving. The photo of a man grabbed her attention. For a moment, her surroundings shifted from an old farmhouse to her parent's store. Her mother lay dead on the floor, and a man stood over her. The man in the picture. She fumbled for her phone to capture his image. Finally, she had evidence but no warrant. Should she, or shouldn't she?

"What took you so long?" Jeannie punched the accelerator. "Zoe left with Daniel a half-hour ago. You know you have to clear your phone of any photos you took at the house, right?"

A tear slid down her cheek. "I know."

DANIEL CROWDED into a booth at Little Joe's Sandwich Shop beside Bernie with Jeannie and Zoe across from them. He hadn't been this close to her since they were locked in an embrace, trying to dodge a bullet or two. This was much nicer. Shoulder to shoulder, hip to hip, knee to knee. This was turning into his favorite restaurant.

"We need to figure this out." Jeannie took a drink. "It's gone on too long, and it's interfering with my life. I'm not spending time with my husband like I want. I miss him."

"He must be a saint," Daniel said. Ouch, that didn't come out right. "I mean, to put up with the hours of a wife who's a detective."

Zoe cleared her throat. "How long have you been married?"

"Twenty-one years," Jeannie said softly.

Burgers arrived, and talk was suspended in favor of filling their stomachs.

Hums of approval sounded around the table.

After fifteen minutes, Daniel pushed his plate to one side. "Where do we begin?"

"Let's talk about who we believe killed Tariq Ghazzi and why," Bernie said. "I'll go first." She opened her phone. "Caleb Pidgeon. So far, he hasn't given us an alibi for that night, and he could have motive."

"What motive?" Jeannie said.

"Revenge for leaving his mother and him. Or they could be in business together, and Ghazzi cheated him. Or Ghazzi is trying to take over the business whatever it is—drugs, guns, whatever."

"I think it's Ursula and Caleb together," Zoe said. "For the insurance money."

"Now, that makes more sense to me." Jeannie wagged a finger in the air. "Mr. FBI man? What do you think?"

"It seems like a very personal murder to me—a crime of passion. I'd look for the person who hated him the most." He stretched, placing his arm along the back of the booth. "Right now, none of the people we're looking at seems right to me."

"There is one." Jeannie tapped the table. "Kabir Nayar. Think about the emails he sent. They were passionate."

"Isn't he the guy who got shot yesterday at the school?" Zoe said. "What does he have to do with Ghazzi's murder?"

"His son was killed on a school outing, and he holds Major/Ghazzi responsible," Bernie said.

"That's an excellent motive." Zoe scanned the group. "Did he have opportunity?"

Bernie pulled up notes on her phone. "We didn't have a chance to check his alibi before he was shot."

"But he's a big guy." Daniel took his arm down and leaned forward. "No way he was the hooded figure I saw in the alley."

"Who's to say the hooded figure is our killer?" Jeannie said.

She had a point. Had he—they—been chasing the wrong clues?

Bernie looked at Jeannie. "I'll talk to Mrs. Nayar."

"We'll go together." Jeannie pushed to her feet. "But

tomorrow. I'm exhausted. See you all in the morning at the precinct."

◁▭▭▭▭▭▭▭▭▭▭▭▭▭▷

BERNIE THREW her purse on her desk, knocking her empty metal travel mug, nameplate, and bowl of peppermints on the floor. She collapsed in the chair and groaned.

"Well, aren't we Miss Grumpy this morning." Jeannie leaned back in her chair, lost her balance, and grabbed for her desk to keep from flipping head over heels.

It was the look on her face that did it—eyebrows arched over bulging eyes and mouth wide open.

A giggle started deep down, and by the time it reached Bernie's lips, a full-blown laugh emerged. "Sorry." She held up her hand as she bent over in spasms of mirth. "I can't seem to stop."

"Glad I could brighten your day." Jeannie's mouth twitched between a scowl and a grin.

Finally under control, Bernie plopped into her chair. "Didn't get much sleep last night. I must be more tired than I thought." She retrieved her mug. "I need more coffee. What's on the agenda today?"

"I thought we'd start with a visit to the hospital to see Kabir and Amber Nayar." She raised an eyebrow at Bernie. "If you think you can stay awake that long."

"I'll even drive."

"Where are we going?" Zoe Poole appeared next to her. Tan camo today. With matching boots.

"*We're* going to the hospital." Jeannie indicated Bernie and herself.

"Good. I need to go see how Ursula is doing." Zoe squared her shoulders.

"Not with us." Jeannie pushed past her. "We'll catch up later."

Bernie frowned. "We're going to the same place."

170

"Sorry." Jeannie glanced at her partner. "You're right. Come on, Ms. Poole."

As they pulled into the parking garage, Jeannie pulled out her phone. "Have you heard from Daniel?"

"No." Part of what had Bernie on edge this morning. She'd tried calling him and got no answer.

"Neither have I. And, his car wasn't in the parking lot when we left. Wonder what he's up to?"

"Maybe he's at the hospital visiting Rose." That nagging irritation she'd felt all morning eased.

"Yeah." Jeannie nodded. "That would make sense."

They exited the elevator on the ICU floor and headed for Nayar's room. Daniel leaned against the man's doorframe. Jeannie hastened over to him.

"He's not here." Daniel stood.

"What do you mean he's not here?" Jeannie entered the room.

"I mean he died, and his body and his wife are gone. Disappeared."

Jeannie stormed off in the direction of the nurse's station.

"I pity the person on the other end of her anger." Daniel winced.

"I should go after her." Bernie gazed down the hall.

"Hang on. I'd like to talk to you." He reached out to her. "That night I told you everything, I—" He dropped his arm. "Never mind. This isn't the time."

"What?" A sudden tightness clenched her chest.

His blue eyes locked on hers. "I feel closer to you than I have to anyone in a very long time."

"I—" Her heart pounded, and her stomach flipped. Was she falling in love?

"Santos." Jeannie's voice sounded next to her. "We need to go. Now."

"Where are you going?" Daniel jogged up next to Jeannie. "I want to help. I have access to resources you don't."

"All right." Jeannie halted and studied him. "But don't get in my way, O'Leary."

"No, ma'am."

Jeannie rounded a corner and slammed into Zoe. "Watch where you're—"

"I've been looking for you." Zoe grabbed Jeannie's arm. "Ursula Pidgeon's been attacked."

"What is it with this hospital? What happened to Pidgeon?"

"The nurse said someone turned off her IV."

"When did this happen?" Jeannie changed direction and headed down another hallway, Zoe by her side.

"It happened during shift change. Somebody turned off the alarm."

Jeannie glanced over her shoulder. "Bernie, call for backup. We need more officers over here."

Bernie tried to yank her phone from her pocket as she raced to keep up. It caught on something. She pulled harder until the device finally broke free. Jeannie rounded a corner and disappeared from sight. Bernie swiveled to look for Daniel. What was he doing?

"Come on. We'll lose Jeannie and Zoe."

On the other side of the wall, her partner talked to a nurse in scrubs. "And you didn't see anything unusual?"

"No." The woman hesitated. "Well, there was a gentleman here earlier."

"What did he look like?"

"I'm not really sure. He had on a long, hooded jacket." She squinted her eyes in concentration. "Navy. Or possibly gray. I thought he was a visitor stretching his legs. He walked around, glancing in all the windows."

"We need to move Ms. Pidgeon to another room. Preferably

on another floor. And put a guard on her 24/7." Bernie looked at the stricken nurse. "Can you help us with that, please?"

"Of course." She disappeared down the hall to the nurse's station.

The four huddled to one side.

"We have two problems. Where is Caleb Pidgeon, and where has Mrs. Nayar taken her husband's body?" Jeannie shifted from one foot to another. "Much as it pains me, I'm asking for your help." She looked at Zoe and Daniel.

"I'm in." Zoe pressed her lips together in a determined line.

Daniel nodded. "Me too."

"You guys search for Caleb. Bernie and I will look for Amber and Kabir. Keep in touch."

<hr/>

"Would Amber take the body of her husband home?" Bernie checked her mirrors before backing out of the parking space en route to the Nayars' home. "I know nothing about East Indian burial customs."

"She's Catholic. I don't know about him." Jeannie pursed her lips. "I need to send a photo of Caleb to Daniel and to Zoe."

"Good idea. We haven't ruled Kabir Nayar out as a suspect in Ghazzi's death, have we?" Bernie signaled for a left turn. "But do you think Amber knew anything about it?"

"He's still a suspect, but I doubt she was in on it. You saw the relationship there."

At the Nayars' home, Bernie pulled into the empty driveway. No cars in the garage, and the curtains were pulled tight on all the windows. "Let's go around back."

Jeannie tried the knob. Unlocked. She cracked the door. "Mrs. Nayar? Detective Jansen of the Pleasant Valley Police Department. Are you home?" Silence. "We need to talk to you. May we come in?" She turned to Bernie. "You all right with a quick walk-through to make sure she's not laying in there hurt?"

"Okay." Bernie paused in the kitchen. Someone had cleaned up the stew on the stove, but the scent lingered in the air. Techs had removed floor tiles where Jeannie's blood had pooled. Memories of that day played across her mind once more.

"In here."

The master bedroom looked as if a storm had hit, with woman's clothing scattered everywhere, luggage pieces strewn about like giant building blocks, and an odd hexagonal box in the middle of the bed.

"What do you suppose that is?" Jeannie said.

"It looks like a lady's hatbox, but it's too tall."

"I guess if the hat had feathers—" Jeannie snapped a photo. "We'll get Bulldog on it. He'll figure it out."

"We need to leave."

The two women walked to their car.

"It looks as if Mrs. Nayar packed a bag in a hurry. I wonder why?" Bernie said.

Jeannie pondered the tiny suburban house. "I have no idea."

"Maybe we need to call the local mortuaries."

"Good thinking. Get someone on it right away."

"And I'll alert the rest of the department to be on the lookout for Mrs. Nayar." Bernie's phone rang in her hand. "Santos." She listened intently, hung up, and turned to meet Jeannie's questioning gaze. "We have another murder."

27

"Don't tell me it's Pidgeon," Jeannie said. "I left Chicago PD to get away from all the murders. We've got to stop this guy, Santos."

"It's not Ursula Pidgeon." Bernie made a U-turn and headed for the north side of town. "It's Olivia Belkin." First Tariq Ghazzi, then Henry Abbott, and now Olivia Belkin. She knew a connection between the men, but Belkin? Where did she fit?

"Ghazzi, Abbott, Belkin. With attempts on O'Leary and Pidgeon. What are we missing?"

Bernie peered at her partner. "Just what I was thinking. Maybe we have two killers. We were already convinced Caleb murdered Abbott. Maybe that one doesn't belong with the others."

"If we take Abbott out of the equation, then what? That removes Caleb as the killer of Ghazzi. And I don't like that," Jeannie said. "He has motive and is the right size to be the hooded figure. Besides, our only other suspect for Ghazzi's murder is Kabir Nayar, and he's dead. So, he couldn't have killed Belkin."

"Okay. We leave Abbott in." Bernie parked at the curb. Gray siding with burgundy shutters and a yellow door. Flowers everywhere. Ms. Belkin had her colorful side, after all. Bernie stuck her hand in her pocket. Her medallion was gone. The sudden feeling of loss caught her off guard. She hadn't realized how much it meant to her until now. *Lord, please help me recover it.*

"You okay?" Jeannie said.

"I'm fine." She pointed to the house. "Let's get to it."

Inside the home, the assistant M.E. knelt beside the body on the bedroom floor. "Blunt force trauma. Just like her boss. Only this time it was a baseball bat." He proffered the murder instrument wrapped in plastic.

"Straight forward? Nothing weird?" Jeannie examined the weapon. "Time of death?"

"You know I—"

"A guess." Jeannie sighed.

Bernie had heard this game played at every murder scene. When would this end? All these people murdered. Why? She stepped into the hall to make room for the stretcher.

"Maybe three hours ago. Give or take an hour."

"Thanks."

"Who found the body?" Bernie watched as they removed the corpse.

Jeannie consulted her notes. "Her son Zachary. They were supposed to meet for lunch. When she didn't show, he came looking for her."

A man of about forty sat on the couch with his elbows on his knees, hands dangling between his legs.

"Mr. Belkin? Our condolences on the death of your mother." Bernie perched on a chair near the couch. His grief looked real.

Jeannie sat behind her.

"I know when she was killed." Zachary Belkin raised his head. "I was on the phone with her when the doorbell rang." Belkin lifted his gaze to the ceiling and gulped. "She said she was expecting a package and hung up." He fixed Bernie with a fierce gaze. "It was her killer, wasn't it?"

"We'll find out who did this." Bernie leaned forward. "What time was your call?"

Zachary blinked. "About two and a half hours ago."

"You've been a big help. This officer will get your formal statement, and again, we're sorry for your loss."

Outside, Bernie and Jeannie surveyed the neighborhood.

"The guys are doing the usual house-to-house," Jeannie said.

"Any luck so far?"

"Most of the neighbors work." Jeannie scowled. "What is it these days? When I was a kid, you couldn't get away with anything. Never thought I'd miss those neighborhood busybodies."

"I know. Where I lived, Mrs.—"

Jeannie's cellphone chimed. "Kabir Nayar's body is at St. Joseph Mortuary. We need to get over there."

Bernie hit the lights and siren.

They brushed past the secretary and presented their badges to the man sitting behind the desk in the office.

"Stop any procedures on Kabir Nayar. Now," Jeannie said.

"By what authority?"

"He's a suspect in a murder case. That makes him a candidate for an autopsy." Jeannie stepped closer. "Stop what you're doing until the necessary paperwork arrives."

The man paled. He punched a button on his phone. "Do nothing to Mr. Nayar."

The door behind them flew open. "No. You must not take him." Mrs. Nayar raced into the room and flung herself at Jeannie. "I beg of you. Let me bury him in peace."

"I'm sorry, Mrs. Nayar." Jeannie guided her to a chair. "We—"

"I will tell you everything you need to know. Kabir is the killer. But please, let me bury him first."

Bernie's heart ached for the woman's agony, but they had no choice. "I'm sorry. We need to take him." Bernie caught the undertaker's eye. "Has the paperwork come through?"

He nodded.

"Please transport his body to our morgue ASAP." She helped Mrs. Nayar to stand. "Let's get your statement."

The woman wrenched herself away from Bernie's grasp. "I will drive myself. I don't need you."

"DETECTIVE SANTOS, there's a guy in the drunk tank claims he's your father." The officer stood in front of her desk, both thumbs hooked in her belt.

Bernie stared at the uniformed officer before her. Relief, anger, and shame fought for control of her tongue. Kindness won. "Thank you. I'll be over in a minute."

"So, he is?"

Bernie nodded.

"Did I hear that right?" Jeannie raised an eyebrow at her.

"It's a long story." One she needed to share with her partner. And she would. Soon. Right now, she had to bail her papá out of jail. "I'll be back."

Gray skies reflected Bernie's mood as she drove home, her father snoring next to her. Rain pelted her windshield, and by the time she managed to half walk, half carry him into the house, they were both soaked.

"Hello, handsome." Squawk.

"Hello, beautiful bird." Victor Santos stumbled across the room to Lori's cage. "Did you miss me?"

"Papá, you must stay here until I get home." Bernie grabbed his face in her hands. "Do you understand me?"

"Of course, daughter." He pushed her hands away. "I may be drunk, but I'm not stupid."

"I know you're not—"

Her front door exploded inward. Bernie threw her father to the floor. She crouched and drew her weapon.

Squawk. "Bad men." Lori jumped between her perch and the side of her cage, screeching at the top of her lungs.

"Lori. Hush. Down." She would not let anything happen to either her father or her bird.

Three men poured in through the opening along with the dampness and pounding of a hard rain.

Bernie opened fire. The small room filled with the acrid smell of gunpowder. One man screamed and grabbed his arm. The other two paused long enough for Bernie to aim. A second man fell to the ground, his knee shattered by her bullet. Rage and frustration erupted from deep within, and she charged over the sofa straight at the attackers. The remaining two disappeared into the gray curtain of water, leaving their comrade to his fate.

Bernie kicked his gun across the room. She aimed her weapon. This was the man who killed her mamá. He deserved to die. She blinked. No. This was not the man. And she was a policewoman. She lowered her arm and knelt beside him.

No parrot chatter reached her ears. Another wave of anger swept through her. She blinked. *Concentrate.*

"Why did you come here?"

"My knee." He groaned.

"Do you want a matching set?" Bernie's stomach turned. She couldn't. She glanced across the room. Where was her father?

Or could she?

He blanched. "We were looking for the old man."

"Papá? Why?"

"He's shooting off his mouth about trying to find who killed his old lady."

"You mean my mother?" Bernie pressed her gun to his other knee and showed him her badge.

"We didn't know." His eyes widened.

"Now you do. Leave my papá alone. He's just an old man." She pressed harder. "Got it?"

He nodded.

"Go tell your buddies." She helped him up. "No more, or I sic the whole police force on you. They don't take kindly to people who threaten police officers."

The man limped out and disappeared.

When she was sure they were gone, Bernie raced around the sofa. She faltered at the sight of her father lying prone on the floor.

"Are they gone?" He raised his head.

"What have you done?" Bernie put an arm under her papá and helped him to the couch.

She crossed the room to her sweet pet. Lori huddled, trembling on the bottom of her cage.

"Oh, no." Bernie put her hand inside the cage and stroked the parrot's chest. "My precious bird."

After a while, Lori stepped onto Bernie's finger and climbed to her forearm. Bernie sat on the couch next to her father and crossed her arms so Lori could snuggle against her chest.

———

DANIEL PULLED into Bernie's drive and rushed from the car. Bernie's earlier call had sounded desperate. Drips from waterlogged trees showered him as he crossed to where her front door lay propped to one side.

He drew his weapon. "Bernie? Are you in there?"

"I'm here." She appeared at the doorway, Lori on her shoulder. "Watch the doorstep and the puddles."

The parrot flew the short distance to perch on Daniel's shoulder. She nuzzled his hair.

"Lori is in need of some TLC after this afternoon."

"I can imagine." Stroking the bird's back, he scrutinized her room. His heart rate quickened. The smell of gunpowder hung in the air along with another familiar smell. Blood. He glanced at a stain on her carpet. Light reflected off bullet casings scattered across the floor.

"Looks like a whole lot of shooting went on here. Are all the good guys okay?"

"Yes."

"What about the bad guys?"

"One has a wounded arm and another a knee he won't be using for a while."

"How many were there?"

Her eyes flashed at him. "Three."

Admiration and fear for her hit him at the same time. He'd almost lost her. But he hadn't. He grabbed her and buried his face in her hair. *Thank you, God.*

She stiffened at first, but after a few seconds, returned his embrace. "I don't know what happened, Daniel. They blew open the door, swarmed it, and I felt like I could have taken on ten men. I was furious. All I wanted to do was kill them."

"I understand." He stroked her hair. "They invaded your home." He caught sight of her father. "Threatened someone you love. But you dug deep and found the control you needed. That's all that matters now." He released her.

"Give us a kiss." Lori touched her beak to Daniel's cheek.

Bernie chuckled. "I think someone is jealous."

"No need. Lori Darling, you'll always be my favorite bird." Daniel rubbed her beak.

"There's something else." She led him to the sofa. "I have a story to tell you, and I need your help."

28

Bernie walked through the condo a second time. Daniel watched as she inspected the safe house he'd found for her and her father.

"What do you think?"

"It's perfect." She stood in the middle of the living room with her hands on her hips. "It's just what we agreed on. Two bedrooms, a kitchen, and a nice living area on the third floor." She walked to the window. "Not too many windows and no balcony." She sighed. "Thank you."

"Good. It's the only one that matches our requirements." He liked the place. Big rooms. High ceilings. Big screen TV.

"There's no phone here, right?"

"No phone. I'm not new at this." He raised an eyebrow. "Your dad should be very comfortable here."

"I know. I'm sorry." She placed a hand on his chest.

"I reached out to some agent friends who are willing to help look after him, but it will be spotty." He covered her hand with his. "Can you get some of your police buddies involved?"

"I haven't said anything at the precinct yet." She removed her hand. "Not even Jeannie."

"You need to, Bernie."

She nodded.

What was he doing? He moved away before she could see her pain mirrored on his face. As soon as he found out who killed Tariq Ghazzi, he'd be returning to Cleveland.

"I need to get back." She looked at him. "Daniel, I—" She stepped closer and lifted her face to his. "Thank you again."

He pressed his lips to hers. Fire shot through him, and he pulled her into his arms.

The key in the lock sounded a split second before the door opened. Daniel and Bernie shot apart. He grabbed a tissue and pretended to blow his nose as Bernie's father and the FBI officer entered the safe house.

Victor Santos eyed first Daniel and then his daughter. "Bernadette?"

"Papá." She crossed to him and gave him a hug. "This is Daniel O'Leary."

"I know Daniel." He raised an eyebrow at her.

"Of course, you do. I forgot. This is a very nice place for us. You'll be safe here. I need to go, but I'll be back tonight." She kissed him on the cheek and left.

<hr>

BERNIE DROVE LIKE AN OLD WOMAN, or how she imagined an old woman drove, to the precinct. What a difference a few days could make. She'd gone from the detective who rode the straight and narrow to the cop who pulled a file without permission, started an investigation on her own, and lied to her partner. She dreaded talking to Jeannie.

How could she ask for help protecting her father? She didn't deserve to be a detective. She should quit right now, take her father, move far away, and work flipping burgers. Squaring her shoulders, she opened the door.

"Santos. Where have you been?" Jeannie's voice carried across the room. "Get over here. We have work to do."

Bernie sat next to Jeannie's desk.

"I'd ask if your puppy died, but you don't have a puppy." Jeannie laid her pencil on the file she was working on. "Your parrot?"

"My neighbors are taking care of her." Bernie looked her partner in the eye. "I have a story to tell you."

People around them came and went. Jeannie took notes and asked questions. When she was finished, Bernie folded her hands in her lap.

"You should have told me." Jeannie loosened her ponytail and ran her hands through her hair before tying it up again. "I would have helped. That's what partners do."

"I'm sorry. I shouldn't have worked on my mother's case without permission." Maybe she'd get suspended but not fired. She had some money saved and would be okay if it wasn't too long.

"Do you really think I care more about following the rules than helping my friends?" Jeannie swiveled her chair toward Bernie. "Or finding the bad guys?" She softened her tone, patted Bernie's arm. "Okay. Don't worry. Now I know, and we'll take care of it. Together. Some of the guys owe me favors. We'll get them to help with staying with your dad until we can catch these scumbags." She picked up her phone.

"Send the picture you took of the photo from Elsa's album to Bulldog, and we'll get him working on an ID." She pressed numbers on her phone and grinned at Bernie. "Come on, Santos. Together we're unbeatable, remember?"

"Yes." Bernie let out a deep breath. No suspension and not fired. *Thank you, Lord.* She smiled. "Thanks, Jeannie."

"No sweat." Jeannie ended a call. "I've got a few guys set up to watch your dad for now. I'll call a couple more later." She picked up the file on her desk. "Believe me. We've got bigger problems to solve. Like two missing people. Caleb Pidgeon and Amber Nayar."

A uniformed officer appeared at the desk. "Captain Yancy wants to see you. Now."

Bernie and Jeannie swiveled their chairs to face the back of the room, where two offices stood side by side. One belonged to the precinct captain, Captain Zubari—who was on his honeymoon. The other belonged to his second in command, Captain Yancy.

"Let's get this over with." Bernie stood and smoothed her pants. After Henry Abbott's murder, Captain Yancy wasn't sure she should be working the case. Now that they had another body, would he remove her? Or worse. Jeannie may not want to demote her, but she didn't know about the captain.

When Jeannie knocked on his door, the man's bald head lifted, and he motioned for them to enter. "Sit." He closed his computer and regarded them with tired eyes. "This is a small town. One murder is bad enough, but three?"

Bernie glanced at Jeannie.

"Do you have any leads? Are we dealing with a serial killer?"

Jeannie opened her mouth to answer.

"This has to stop." Captain Yancy thrust a finger at them. "And if you can't get results, I'll have to find someone else who can." He leaned back. "Tell me what you've got."

"We're still not sure that one person committed all the crimes. But we've narrowed our suspect list to two people," Jeannie said.

"Good. Bring them in for questioning."

Bernie and Jeannie shared a look of understanding. How did they explain that one of their suspects was not only dead, but missing? Better to agree and get on with the job of solving these cases.

"Yes, sir." Jeannie rose.

Back at their desks, Bernie turned on her computer. "Zoe and Daniel are looking for Caleb Pidgeon. Have you heard anything yet?"

"No, but I didn't expect to."

"Why are we still looking for Mrs. Nayar? I thought she came in to give us a statement."

"She never showed." Jeannie squinted at her computer screen.

"Any ideas where to begin looking?"

"That's what I've been doing for the past hour."

Mission Impossible sounded from under a pile of papers. Jeannie tossed them aside and grabbed her cellphone.

"Jansen. Got it. We're on our way." She caught the arm of her chair as she stood and removed her purse. "Ms. Pidgeon is awake."

Seven minutes of lights and sirens later, Jeannie jerked the car to a stop outside the main entrance to the hospital. She put the police sign in the window and got out. The elevator opened on a huddle of nurses. As Bernie and Jeannie approached, they spread into a semicircle.

Something wasn't right.

"We're here to see Ursula Pidgeon," Jeannie said.

The nurses exchanged glances.

A male in his forties stepped forward. "Detective, after we called you, I went in to give Ms. Pidgeon her meds, and she wasn't there."

"Where is she?" Jeannie glared at him.

A freckled-faced young woman raised her hand. "I saw Ms. Pidgeon in a transport wheelchair headed for CT scanning about an hour ago."

"I think I need to take over." Bernie motioned Jeannie over to the side and gave her a stern look. "Too many deaths, too many people lost on your watch, and too little sleep has you at the end of your rope."

"I—" Jeannie stared at her. "I think you're right, and that's why we make a good team, Santos."

They returned to the nurses.

"Where is the officer outside her door? We need to speak to him," Bernie said.

"He told us he'd been called back to the station," an older nurse said.

"Would you check on that?" Bernie caught Jeannie's eye and turned her attention back to the nurses. "Would one of you check to see if Ms. Pidgeon made it to CT and if she might still be there?" Bernie tapped notes on her phone.

"Right away." The older nurse hustled off.

"Did any of you see anyone or anything else that looked out of the ordinary today?"

"There was a hooded character got off the elevator this morning," the male nurse said. "When he caught sight of me, he got back on and left. I figured he got off on the wrong floor."

"Can you describe him?"

"Medium height. Couldn't see his face. Dark gray hooded jacket."

"Thanks."

The older nurse returned. "Ms. Pidgeon wasn't scheduled for CT today. They haven't seen her."

29

At the precinct, Bernie stared at her computer screen. So many lies and lives to untangle. Her stomach churned. She'd told a few of her own and realized how easy it was to justify bending the truth in the name of a good cause. But was it worth it in the end?

An officer approached Jeannie's desk. "Ma'am, they need Dr. O'Leary in autopsy."

She nodded. "I'll call him."

"I hate to pull Daniel away from searching for Caleb," Bernie said. "Especially since I'm almost certain it was Caleb who got Ursula out of the hospital."

"I agree. We find one, and we'll probably find the other." Jeannie leaned back and threw her pencil on the desk. "But since Rose is in the hospital, Daniel's our acting M.E., and it's important for him to do the autopsy on Kabir Nayar. Zoe will have to search on her own."

"I think we need to switch our attention to Caleb. He's still a Person of Interest. We suspect he killed Henry Abbott, and he may have been the one shooting at Daniel."

"But I don't want to forget about Amber Nayar. She claimed

her husband killed Ghazzi, and she would give us a statement."
Jeannie crossed her arms on her desk. "We need to talk to her."

"Give her some time. She's grieving." Bernie played with the
ring on her right hand. "She'll come in."

<hr>

DANIEL BUMPED over the curb into the police parking lot.
Bernie's car was in her designated spot. More unfinished
business. His feelings for her grew stronger every day. Had he
forgotten how to pray? It'd been a long time. He pushed the
power button on his rental car and sat in the silence before
walking into the autopsy suite.

"Where's our patient?"

"I've prepared him for you over here, Doctor." Rose's
assistant stood next to a shrouded figure. "Would you like me to
help?"

"Of course." Daniel smiled. "You probably know more about
this than I do." He snapped gloves over his hands. "Shall we
begin?"

An hour later, Daniel sat at his aunt's desk, reading through
the notes on Kabir Nayar's autopsy. He was right. There were a
couple of surprises. One thing for sure. Kabir didn't kill Tariq
Ghazzi.

<hr>

"YOU'RE SURE ABOUT THIS?" Bernie laid the paper onto the
desk.

"He's too tall." Daniel gathered the file together.

Bernie sat next to Jeannie in Rose O'Leary's office. Amber
Nayar had told them her husband killed Tariq Ghazzi, and if
Nayar was their killer, they could close at least one murder case.
But facts proved otherwise. The blow to Ghazzi's head signified
a much shorter assailant.

"The part I don't understand is that Kabir died of asphyxiation. I thought it was from complications due to the shooting."

"The docs had him on high doses of morphine. It wouldn't have taken much to put a pillow over his face and finish him off." Daniel shrugged. "He never would have wakened."

"The only person in the room with him consistently was his wife." Bernie shuddered.

"Don't look at me like that." Jeannie folded her arms across her chest. "I know." She flashed angry eyes. "Could you blame her? He beat her."

Bernie blinked to clear her own eyes. "You know that's no excuse for murder."

"Don't forget, Ursula Pidgeon was on the same floor." Jeannie's face lit up. "If Caleb snuck in to visit his sister, he could have waited for a chance to murder Kabir."

"Possible. But what would be his motive?"

"We won't know until we catch up to him."

"But, I agree." Jeannie sighed. "It looks like Amber Nayar killed Kabir." She straightened. "We still don't know who murdered Ghazzi or Abbott or Belkin." She waved her arms. "I still think it's Caleb. He's into something nasty. Maybe some of the school personnel were in on his schemes. Any reports of drug activity at the school?"

"I don't know." Daniel rubbed the back of his neck. "Could be. I'll check."

"You're from Cleveland," Jeannie said. "What would you know about Pleasant Valley?"

Bernie leaned in. "Daniel has more experience dealing with drug dealers than we have."

"Sorry." Jeannie's gaze dropped to her hands.

"Apology accepted." Daniel studied Jeannie for a moment. "I know how hard it is to accept help from outside. But since you've known my true identity, you've let me be a part of your investigation, and I thank you."

A smile rose from Bernie's heart to her lips and warmed her soul. She gazed at Daniel, who gave her a quick smile.

Jeannie cleared her throat. "That was—that was the nicest acceptance I've ever received." She sighed. "Okay. If not drugs, then what other motive could there be?"

"Despite what I said earlier about it being a crime of passion, Ghazzi may have crossed the wrong people, and they decided to get rid of him." He leaned back. "And I became the perfect fall guy."

"But why?"

"Who knows?" Daniel frowned. "We'll have to ask Caleb."

Bernie's mind kept tripping on something said earlier. What was it?

"You've been quiet." Jeannie looked at her.

"I don't think either of those theories is correct." Bernie shook her head. "Something is nagging at me. Can we go over how they're related to each other again?"

Jeannie sighed. "Tariq Ghazzi and Ursula Pidgeon were stepbrother and sister, and the parents of Caleb Pidgeon. Ursula Pidgeon also was Ghazzi's personal assistant at the school."

"Henry Abbott was brother to Elsa Abbott who's sleeping with Caleb Pidgeon. Henry was also brother to Irene Abbott who was girlfriend to Ghazzi. Irene was killed in a raid in Cleveland." Daniel jotted on his notepad. "And, Henry Abbott worked as a teacher where Ghazzi was the headmaster."

"Amber and Kabir Nayar had a son Denis who attended the school where Ghazzi, Abbott, Pidgeon, and Olivia Belkin worked. Denis was killed in a bus accident on a school trip."

"That's part of what's bothering me." Bernie snapped her fingers. "What about Olivia Belkin? Why was she killed? Do you honestly think she would have been part of a terrorist group? Or if it is one of these HVEs, would she be part of one of those?"

"Maybe she found out about it and threatened to go to the police."

Then it came to her in a flash of clarity. Could the solution be that simple? Bernie scooted to the end of her chair.

"You once said to me a mother will do almost anything to protect her child. And if something happens to him, look out."

Jeannie nodded. "But that's when I suspected Ursula Pidgeon of killing Ghazzi over their son, Caleb."

"We have another mother in the mix. And something *did* happen to her child."

30

"Back to Amber Nayar again?" Jeannie tilted her face to the ceiling and let out a heavy sigh.

"Hear me out." Bernie placed a hand on the desk. "The Nayars lost the civil case against the school. They had no other legal recourse. Their son was dead, killed by what they called the devil, and they could do nothing about it."

"She couldn't have killed those people. You saw her. She's the victim of abuse. She's weak and beaten down." Jeannie reached a hand toward Bernie.

"Yes. And I read what Randy found out. She was an Olympic hopeful in her country when she was young. Track and field. She used to exercise to help her with her grief." Bernie made a muscle. "She's strong, Jeannie. And she's fast. I saw how she fought against the officers in the house the day we were looking for Kabir."

"I know you have a soft spot for this woman, Jeannie," Daniel said. "But Bernie makes sense."

"Okay." Jeannie drew in a breath. "I get Ghazzi and Belkin and Pidgeon because they're front line. They would be responsible for decisions that affect the children. But how do you explain Abbott?"

"Abbott was the driver of the van." Bernie held up Randy's report. "I read that in Bulldog's report as well."

"But she said she saw a white truck."

"She may have. Maybe Caleb did visit Abbott, and she took advantage of that to throw us off. Or he may have killed Abbott." Bernie touched her pocket. "But my money's on Amber."

◁━━━━━━━━━━▷

HER MEDALLION. Daniel dug it out of his pants pocket.

"I've been meaning to get this to you. I saw you drop it at the hospital the other day and keep forgetting to return it." He handed her the silver disc.

She ran her fingers over the words engraved on the metal and raised damp eyes to his. "Thank you."

He offered her a box of tissues and knew one thing for certain. He loved her. But how could they ever make this work?

"I'm glad you got it back, Santos. Maybe you'd say a prayer for me." Jeannie rose. "In the meantime, we have a woman to question."

"You have no idea how much this—" Bernie stood, "means to me." She patted her pocket.

"You're welcome. I'll call the safe house and check on your dad. Be there in a minute."

She gave him that smile that made him forget where he was and what he was doing. He blinked and punched in the number. No answer. He dialed again. Nothing.

He punched in another number. "I need you to get over to the safe house ASAP. Call me back." Within five minutes, his phone rang. His heart pounded as he listened. "Okay. Get an ambulance and forensics there, and keep me posted."

Better to get it over with. He walked toward Bernie. As he grew closer, his pace increased until he was running. "We've got a problem."

Her heart-shaped face with those brown eyes and full lips tilted toward his. So vulnerable, and yet her square shoulders and straight back spoke to her underlying strength. She could handle his news.

"The gang found the safe house. They overcame the officers on guard and snatched your father."

SHE SAGGED IN HER CHAIR. When her father had been set up in the safe house, she'd feared news like this. But, as the hours passed, she'd grown confident, believing he was safe, and she could devote all her energy to the cases.

Now, after the attack on her home, the disappearance of yet another key person, and the discoveries based on Kabir Nayar's autopsy, her father's disappearance almost broke her. Gathering her strength, she forced her spine into alignment and rose.

She felt the familiar form of the medallion once more. "Let's go."

"Not without me." Jeannie grabbed her jacket. "Those were my officers. This is my war too."

Bernie led the way to the police car. *We need Your guidance, Lord.*

"We'll find him." Daniel squeezed her shoulder and retrieved a simple cross from under his shirt, hanging from a sturdy chain around his neck. "I decided I needed my own reminder that we're not alone."

"It's beautiful." Bernie swallowed hard. Maybe they'd find her father alive and well after all.

For once, Bernie was thankful for Jeannie's high-speed driving. Her mind crawled with questions. As soon as she'd follow one, another would cross her path, and she'd be off in another direction.

"Are you all right?" Jeannie touched her arm.

"I can't think straight. It's driving me crazy."

"You need a clear head, Santos."

"Don't make me leave." Bernie's stomach heaved. "He's my father."

"I'm not. Try to calm down and look at this like any other crime scene."

How could she calm down? She closed her eyes and took a deep breath. *The Lord is My Shepherd* ...

"We're here." Jeannie slammed the car into park.

The safe house was on the third floor. Whoever had taken her father had brought him down via the elevator or the steps. "I'll take the stairs up. You guys take the elevator."

"I'm with you." Daniel moved behind her.

"We'll go up on either side. Slowly."

Half-way up, she stopped. Scuff marks. And blood. Tears pooled behind her eyes. "We'll need the forensics team up here."

"I'll call them." He put his hand on her waist. "Only a little farther."

She nodded and continued climbing the staircase.

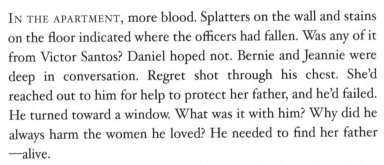

IN THE APARTMENT, more blood. Splatters on the wall and stains on the floor indicated where the officers had fallen. Was any of it from Victor Santos? Daniel hoped not. Bernie and Jeannie were deep in conversation. Regret shot through his chest. She'd reached out to him for help to protect her father, and he'd failed. He turned toward a window. What was it with him? Why did he always harm the women he loved? He needed to find her father —alive.

"Doctor O'Leary?" A young officer said. "Detectives Jansen and Santos need you in the hall."

He hadn't noticed they'd left the apartment. Daniel joined the detectives.

"This lady lives down the hall. She saw the two men who abducted my father. She can give descriptions." A light sheen of sweat shone on Bernie's cheeks. "And she followed them to the street and got a description of the car."

He nodded at the woman, cleared his throat, and tried to steady his voice. "Terrific." *Thank you, God.*

"One of them sounds similar to the man who broke into my house—the one I didn't shoot. They shouldn't be too hard to find." Bernie gave him a pinched smile.

"We put out a BOLO for the car. Waiting to hear back." Jeannie slapped her notepad shut. "Thank you, ma'am." She shook the neighbor's hand.

Jeannie's phone rang as the elevator arrived. She held up a hand for them to wait. Her face turned ashen, and her eyes darted toward Bernie. "Got it."

Daniel's mouth tasted sour.

31

"Jeannie, what is it?" Bernie struggled to breathe.

Daniel wrapped his arm around her waist for support.

"They've found a man that fits the description of your father."

Her legs gave way.

Daniel helped her to a chair. "Is he—?"

"No. But he's beaten up pretty bad." Jeannie said. "We need to get to the hospital."

Her poor frail father. At least she'd have him back and a chance of survival. Depending on how badly he'd been hurt. But could she stand it if he were returned to her only to die? Maybe it wasn't her father.

One way or the other, she needed to know. "Let's go."

———◆———

IN THE HOSPITAL ROOM, Bernie stared at a man who was covered with white gauze and bruises. His eyes were closed. "Papá?" Bernie whispered in his ear.

The man's right eye opened a slit. "*Mija.*" The word came as a puff of breath from between cracked lips.

Tears streamed from her eyes. *Thank You, Jesus.* "You rest now. I love you, Papá."

Daniel handed her a tissue from a box nearby.

"Give me one of those." Jeannie tapped him on the arm.

In the hallway, Bernie rubbed her arms. "I need to stay here for a while. Is there anything I can do from here?"

"Daniel, check in with Zoe and see if she's had any luck locating Caleb." Jeannie pointed to Bernie. "You can call Bulldog and see if he's been able to identify the man in the photo." She bit her lip. "I'll see if there's any news about Amber Nayar or Ursula. We'll meet back here in a few minutes."

Bernie walked back into her father's hospital room. He looked shrunken and helpless. Hot tears of anger stung her eyes. How could anyone do this? First her mamá and now her papá. Someone should pay. Bernie returned to the hall. Her fingers hovered over her cell phone. The man in the photo had killed her mother. And may be responsible for putting her father in the hospital. She punched the buttons. All she wanted was a name.

"Bulldog?"

"Hi, Bernie. I heard about your dad. How is he?"

She brushed her fingers against his door. "He's in bad shape, but he's a fighter." She turned. "Have you been able to find a name for the man in the photo I sent you?"

"Yes. Isaac West."

A spark of excitement shot through her. "Did you find an address?"

"Not anything specific. I believe he's in Cincinnati. That's about it."

"Thanks, Randy." He'd given her more than enough. She knew how to get the rest.

When she hung up, she eased into her father's room and stood once more by his bedside. His chest rose and fell beneath the sheet. He appeared relaxed. She slipped the round piece of metal from her pocket, gripped it in her right hand, and touched her father's arm with the fingertips of her free hand.

"I'm getting close, Papá," her voice came out so soft she wasn't sure she'd spoken the words aloud.

A soft knock brought Bernie to full alert. She glanced at her father sleeping peacefully and opened the door.

"How's your dad?" Jeannie kept her voice low.

"He's good. Resting." Bernie slid through the door and joined her and Daniel in the hallway. "The nurses are taking good care of him."

"I thought we'd check in." Jeannie looked at Daniel. "You first."

"Zoe's not answering." Daniel said. "I'm concerned."

"What about Bulldog? Any luck?"

Should she tell them? Finding her mother's killer was her war. Jeannie had enough to contend with, and Daniel—he was going back to Cleveland after they found Ghazzi's killer.

But if she said nothing, she was no better than Daniel with all his lies.

"The man's name is Isaac West. Last known to be living somewhere near Cincinnati."

"At least that's something." Jeannie paced a short distance away. "Nothing new on the whereabouts of Amber or Ursula."

"I think we should bring Elsa in. She might lead us to Caleb and Ursula and know West's address. We'd take care of two lines of inquiry at the same time." Bernie's pulse quickened.

Elsa held the key she needed. One more bit of information and she'd have him—the man who stole her mother from her all those years ago.

"Yeah, but we need to focus on finding Amber Nayar too." Jeannie took off for the elevator. At the doors, she turned. "Daniel, you take an officer and run out to Elsa's farm. I'll go back to the precinct and ramp up the search for Amber."

"I can go with Daniel." Bernie's stomach rolled. She had to speak with Elsa. "My father's resting and in good hands here."

Jeannie studied her. "Okay. But don't take too long. Got it?"

"Got it." She only hoped Daniel wouldn't get in her way.

As they left the hospital, Bernie fast-walked to the car. In her mind, Elsa held the key to the murder of Henry Abbott and to Bernie's mother's as well. And if they solved those, the others might fall into place—along with who beat up Bernie's father.

Daniel jogged after Bernie. "Slow down, will you?"

"Sorry. What happened to my father has me on edge."

"It would."

Once in the car, Bernie tapped the steering wheel in a nervous rhythm. "Do you think Elsa will be able to tell us West's address?"

"Hard to say. It looks like an old family photo. She may know the people in it. She may not." He brushed her hair from her face. "Is that what's been bothering you?"

She started. "Bothering me? Nothing's been bothering me. Unless you want to count my poor papá being beat to within an inch of his life."

"I'm sorry. I meant besides that. I felt like—never mind. It's not important."

"I'm sorry I snapped at you." Bernie swung the car onto the dirt driveway leading to Elsa's farmhouse and stopped. Staring straight ahead, she swiped at her cheeks. "After this is all over, we need to have a serious talk. But right now, I need to concentrate on what I'm doing. I hope you understand."

"I do." He stroked her hair.

She put the car in gear and started up the drive. Only to slam on the brakes as Zoe appeared in front of her.

32

Bernie dialed Jeannie. "Zoe found them." She kept her voice low even though there was still a quarter-mile of dirt driveway to the farmhouse.

"Them?" Jeannie said.

"She drove to Elsa's to look for Caleb, and while she was waiting, a car pulled up with Amber and Ursula. Amber called out for Caleb and Elsa to help get Ursula into the house. Amber had a shotgun, Jeannie. Now she has them hostage. Zoe was walking away from the house in order to call it in when Daniel and I got here."

"Don't do anything. We're on our way. I mean it. Don't. Do. Anything."

"Got it." Bernie pressed *End* and swiveled on the car seat to face Zoe. "What can you tell me about today?"

"After searching all the places Daniel and I had considered, I decided to stake out Elsa's farm," Zoe said. "I had a hunch Caleb might show up here. The other car appeared before I could take a real look around." A line etched between her brows. "Who is that woman, anyway?"

"She's our chief suspect in Tariq Ghazzi's murder, Amber

Nayar. We believe she may have killed Ms. Belkin as well and been responsible for the attempt on the life of Ursula Pidgeon."

"Those poor people." Zoe stared up the lane toward the farmhouse. "They don't stand much of a chance, do they?"

Daniel met Bernie's eyes. "It's a good thing you spotted them."

"Yeah. We're here now, and backup is on the way." Bernie glanced in the rearview mirror at the solemn face of the private investigator. She yearned to tell her everything would be okay, but ... Motion in her mirrors caught her eye. A car approached. "Daniel, please stay here with Zoe."

Bernie trotted down the dirt road to intercept Jeannie's car. "There's only one way to approach the farm as far as we can tell. Where's the rest of the team?"

"Right behind me."

"We need to leave it clear for backup when they arrive." She motioned for Jeannie to pull off the road. "I'll do the same."

"Everybody have vests?" Jeannie peered around the group. "I don't want anybody taking any chances. Got it? We'll move in close for a look and wait for help."

They spread out and approached the house.

Thank God for brush and trees. Bernie scrutinized the exterior of the house through her binoculars. No movement behind curtains.

"Where is Rambo woman?" Jeannie appeared at her shoulder. "Zoe, whatever."

"She was here a minute ago." Bernie had been too busy studying the scene to notice. "Daniel, have you seen Zoe?"

"No, but I'll look around."

"I've called her twice, and she doesn't answer." Jeannie lowered her binoculars.

A premonition crawled over Bernie's soul. "She was pretty upset when I told her about Amber Nayar. You don't think—?"

Jeannie glared at the house before them. "If she did, she disobeyed a direct order. I'll have her license—after we save her."

"Save who?" Daniel rejoined them.

"We think Zoe may have attempted to rescue the hostages on her own and got captured—or worse." Bernie nodded toward the house. "Otherwise, she would be here with us right now."

"How many hostages does that make?" Daniel shook his head.

"Elsa, Ursula, Caleb, and Zoe. Four."

The three law officers faced the faded exterior of the farmhouse.

"When can we expect backup?" Daniel said.

"The state police are backing us up on this one. They said about ten minutes." Bernie put the binoculars to her eyes again.

"Ten minutes too long for you." A woman's voice sounded behind them.

All three swiveled and reached for their weapons.

"I wouldn't." Amber Nayar aimed a double-barreled shotgun at the center of the group. "Toss your guns into the bushes to my right." The three obliged. "Now your other weapons. The ones on your ankle or at your back." Amber flicked the tip of the shotgun up and down.

Jeannie and Bernie relinquished their backup weapons.

"I don't have a second gun." Daniel lifted his pants legs and turned around.

She motioned them into the yard. As they moved ahead of Amber, a commotion sounded behind Bernie. She turned to see Jeannie gripping the barrel of the shotgun.

As Amber Nayar wrenched the weapon back and forth, Jeannie's hands slipped. Nayar pulled the trigger, and a boom shattered the air. Still Jeannie held on. The two women fell to the ground. Daniel rushed to the tangle of arms and legs. He grabbed the gun, and tore it from Amber Nayar's grasp.

Bernie flipped Nayar onto her back and handcuffed her while Daniel helped Jeannie sit.

"Are you okay?" he said?

She nodded. "How is she?"

Amber Nayar sat hunched in an awkward position.

"Switch her handcuffs around to the front." Jeannie lowered herself to the ground in front of the woman.

Bernie joined her.

"I thought this would get rid of the pain." Amber's body shook. Tears soaked her blouse. "But it hasn't."

"Revenge only multiplies pain. I know from experience," Jeannie said.

Amber's face had aged ten years in the last few days. "What will happen to me?"

"That's for the court to decide." Bernie fought to hold her tears.

"You two take care of Nayar. I'll go free the hostages," Daniel headed to the farmhouse.

"No." Amber struggled against her cuffs, her eyes wide with fear. "There's a bomb."

Bernie raced to catch him. "Daniel. Stop."

The force of the explosion knocked him to the ground. He jumped to his feet, working his jaw to clear his ears. Bernie sat near him, ears ringing. She was okay. Jeannie and Amber huddled a few feet away, staring at the house.

Fire licked at the windows. Four people trapped inside. Daniel ran to the pond. After drenching his shirt, he covered his head before heading for the front door.

"Daniel, no." She had to stop him. She could hear the sirens. Help was close.

He kicked open the door and barged in.

Bernie paced back and forth in front of the house. The familiar whoop of sirens sounded coming up the lane. Anyone inside was most likely dead. And he could be too. The firemen were almost there. They were the trained professionals, not an FBI agent.

She loved him. She closed her eyes.

Lord, please bring him out of the burning fire safely and unharmed.

Daniel staggered out of the house with Ursula over his

shoulders. Bernie raced to his side. The sound of the fire like a giant beast crushing the old wood of the farmhouse between its jaws sounded in her ears, and the intense heat of the flames pushed against her back. She supported Daniel down the porch steps to the yard. After laying Ursula on the grass, he dropped to his knees and coughed violently. Soot blackened phlegm ran from his nose and mouth.

Zoe appeared in the doorway with Elsa draped over her back. She coughed so hard that Elsa slipped from her grasp. Bernie ran to help, but a fireman and EMT made it there first. Daniel and Ursula were being treated by paramedics. She could relax. She scanned the area for Jeannie and Amber.

Where were they? She walked farther into the yard. Jeannie wouldn't have left without her. A disturbance in the pond caught her eye. Bernie jogged toward the water. Dear God. No. Why was Jeannie in the pond? She couldn't swim.

"Help. I need help here." Bernie raced toward the water. At the edge, she stopped long enough to take off her heavy shoes, vest, and her phone. She waded in until the water was too deep. Where was Jeannie? She hadn't seen her for seconds. There. Her partner's head appeared above the water, gasping for breath.

With strong strokes, Bernie swam to where she'd last seen her. She dove into the murky water, waving her arms. Her fingers brushed against fabric. She grabbed and missed. Impossible to see. Bernie waved her arms and legs frantically, hoping to make contact with her drowning friend. A hand clutched hers, nails biting into her palm in desperation. Bernie yanked her to the surface. Jeannie's head broke into the evening air. She gasped, fighting for life-giving oxygen.

Jeannie spurted. "Amber's down there."

"You can't save her." Bernie flipped Jeannie onto her back and swam to shore. "You tried your best."

Swimmers met her halfway to shore.

"There's a woman still in there." Bernie continued with Jeannie back to land. "I need an EMT over here. Now."

Jeannie shivered. The paramedics examined her and wrapped her in a wool blanket. But Jeannie's teeth still chattered.

"You are an amazing person and a great cop, Jeannie Jansen, and I'm proud to call you my partner and my friend." Bernie sat next to her and pulled her close.

Through clicking teeth, Jeannie growled at Bernie. "Don't go getting mushy on me, Santos." But her smile warmed her eyes.

DANIEL DRANK a quart of water before feeling close to normal. He checked on Ursula in the ambulance. Possibly another coma. Blood pressure low. Some new cuts and bruises, but alive. Zoe sat propped against a police car, taking deep breaths. EMTs worked on getting an IV into Elsa. State police mingled with local cops. Where were Bernie and Jeannie?

Police marked off areas of interest with crime scene tape. Forensics worked debris fields beginning with the farthest away. Firetrucks, ambulances, and patrol cars were parked at odd angles. And then he saw the two women, sitting on the edge of the pond. What happened? He took a step in their direction.

What felt like a giant hand smacked him to the ground a second before the sound assaulted his ears.

33

D aniel covered his head and curled into a ball. Pieces of debris rained on his body. He cried out as a nail pierced his upper arm. He pulled it out and tossed it aside. Blood filled the hole and ran down his arm. He lifted his head, keeping his face protected. Zoe lay under a police car. A policeman and EMT shielded Elsa. Pieces of wood and metal covered the ground. Along with nails and ball bearings. The taste of metal in his mouth and the acrid smell of TNT.

The barn had disappeared. All that was left was a shallow hole in the ground. Caleb was a bomb maker, and the barn housed his lab. Daniel got to his feet. His frantic gaze sought Bernie and Jeannie. Where were they?

An EMT guided him to an ambulance. "Let's see about that arm. How's your hearing?"

———————

AT THE SOUND of the blast, Bernie had thrown herself over Jeannie. The ground shook, but very little shrapnel reached their location on the banks of the pond. Destruction behind them.

"Another bomb?" Bernie scanned the scene for Daniel's

familiar form. She spotted him getting checked out once more by EMTs. A pang of concern gripped her heart. She turned her attention to Jeannie. "That was very brave—to try to save Amber Nayar. Especially since you can't swim. You could have drowned."

"And almost did if it hadn't been for you." Jeannie glanced at her. "By the way, thanks for—"

"No need."

A sound from the pond. The women stilled as a team of police divers surfaced in the shallow water with Amber Nayar and carried her body onto the bank.

"You did your best."

"Somehow, it doesn't help right now." Jeannie's voice cracked.

Bernie squeezed her hand.

"No." Her partner pulled away. "Haven't you wondered why that woman got to me?"

"We all have some cases that hit us for no apparent reason." Bernie shrugged. "I just thought this was one of those."

"That's not it." Jeannie drew her blanket tighter. "I was married before. Before Bill. To a cop in Chicago. He beat me. Badly. Then he'd apologize. I loved him, so I'd take him back. Until the last time. I was pregnant with our first child. He hit me in the stomach so hard I lost my baby. And something snapped. I managed to get away from him." Jeannie wiped her face with the blanket.

Bernie didn't know what to say.

"I know. It's a lot to lay on you." She drew in a deep breath. "But now you understand why Amber Nayar touched a nerve with me."

"Jeannie, I'm—"

"I know, Santos."

The two women leaned in, shoulder to shoulder, supporting each other for a brief moment.

"You need to go to the hospital and let a doctor look you over."

"Forget that. I've had my fill of hospitals." Jeannie straightened. "Get me some dry clothes and back to work." She nodded toward her car. "I carry a spare set now."

"I'll get them. Wait here." Bernie jogged to Jeannie's car. Elsa lay on an ambulance gurney in her path. She stopped by the woman's side.

———————————

DANIEL PUSHED the EMT's arm aside. Why was Bernie leaning over Elsa? She was showing the woman something on her phone.

"Sir, I need to look in your eyes."

"Sorry." Daniel focused on the young EMT.

"You seem to be okay. But if you experience any headaches, dizziness ..."

"I'm a doctor. I know what to look for." Daniel smiled to take the sting out of his words.

The man tidied up. "Yes, sir."

Where was Bernie? Daniel rolled his sleeves down and strolled away from the ambulance.

"Have you seen Bernie?" Jeannie tromped across the yard, wrapped in her blanket. "I sent her to get my clothes twenty minutes ago, and she never came back."

Daniel's stomach churned. The doors to Elsa's ambulance closed in preparation for leaving the scene. He bolted over to it and pounded on the back door.

"What's up?"

"I need to speak to Ms. Abbott."

"You can try, but I've given her a sedative. I'm not sure how coherent she'll be."

"It's important." Daniel climbed up next to Elsa. He gently shook her. "Elsa, I need to ask you something."

She tried to focus on his face. "You're cute. Are you married?" She snorted. "Who cares, really?"

213

"Elsa, remember Bernie, the lady cop who showed you a picture on her phone?"

"Is she your girlfriend?"

"No, Elsa. All I need to know is what you told her."

Her eyes widened. "She's going to find my Uncle Isaac for me. So, he can come see me in the hospital."

"Where is he?"

She squinted and pursed her lips. "Cincinnati. Lower Price Hill?" Her eyes closed. "Can't remember." Her head dropped to one side and her eyes closed.

Daniel left the ambulance and closed the door.

"What was that all about?" Jeannie narrowed her eyes at him.

Should he call in his people? He steepled his hands in front of his face.

"I'm speaking to you." She raised her voice. "This is my partner we're talking about."

"I heard you. I'm thinking."

"Well, think out loud, so I can be a part of it." She lifted her arms in the air. Her blanket slipped to the ground.

"Bernie stopped to talk to Elsa. She showed her a photo on her phone. Afterward, she took off." He removed his cellphone from his pocket. "I'm afraid she's gone after her mother's killer on her own."

Jeannie uttered a mild curse and went for her phone—before remembering she'd had it with her when she went into the lake. "Call Bulldog and see if he's found out anything yet. Please."

Daniel listened as Bernie's phone went to voicemail once more. "All right." He punched in the number for the research department at the police station.

"Would you put it on speaker?" Jeannie said.

Daniel punched the appropriate button. "Bulldog, what exactly did you tell Bernie about the man in the photo?

"His name is Isaac West. He's Elsa's father's half-brother. Spent a lot of time at the farm." Bulldog said. "He's been in jail for burglary and assault. But nothing recent. No known address."

"And you told all this to Bernie this afternoon?"

"Yep."

"Great." Jeannie stared at the ground. "Listen, I need you to track Bernie's phone. Call us back on this number as soon as you find her."

"I'll get to work on it right now."

"That's why she was so keen on talking to Elsa." Jeannie said. "She's going after her mother's killer."

"I only hope we're not too late to stop her." A sharp pain hit Daniel in his chest, right where he his heart lay.

34

Bernie's cousin worked for the electric company in Cincinnati. In billing. One call and she had Isaac West's address.

She pulled to the curb and scanned Isaac West's neighborhood. An older woman rocked on a front porch three doors up from where she was parked. Across the street and farther away, three teenagers slouched against a dim streetlight. She focused on the West home.

Was he alone? Only one car in the drive. Lights on behind thin curtains. According to her cousin, his name was the only one listed on the records. She took her folding baton from her purse and stuffed it into an inside pocket of her jacket.

She beeped the car locked and walked to the door. Inside this house lived the man who'd murdered her mother and had beaten her father so badly that he may die as well. Rage swelled inside her. She reached for the picture she'd brought with her, fingers brushing against her medallion. Realization punched her in the stomach.

What was she doing? She came here to kill another human being for the sake of revenge, making her no better than Amber Nayar. She was a policeman. Sworn to uphold the law—to protect and serve. Not just some of the people, but all of them. *God, forgive me.*

She turned and stepped off the porch, headed for her car. Better to question West with the proper backup. Do things by the book.

The door opened, pouring light onto the concrete walk. "You here to see me or inspect my door?" He moved closer.

She swiveled. One look at his face, and she was that 12-year-old girl again. Once more, he towered over her, a smoking gun in his hand, and her mother lay bleeding on the floor.

"Lady. What's with you?" The rasp of his voice brought her back to reality.

"I'm—" Bernie gulped. She extracted her warrant card. "I'm Detective Bernadette Santos. I came to inform you that your niece, Elsa Abbott, is in the hospital in Pleasant Valley in serious condition. She'd like to see you."

"Santos." His eyes narrowed. "I know that name. You're not here to tell me about my niece." He grabbed her with both hands and dragged her across the threshold. Once inside, he held her with one hand while he fished her gun out of its holster with the other. He kicked the door shut with a booted foot. Then he tossed her across the room like a bag of garbage.

Bernie slammed into the wall and slumped to the floor. Anger hardened into resolve. She wanted this man to pay for her parents, but it would be by the book. If she could persuade him to see Elsa, they could bring him in for questioning.

"You're wrong. Elsa's farmhouse exploded, and she was injured. She asked me to let you know."

"Oh, dear." Isaac West twisted his face into a grotesque caricature of sympathy. "Poor little Elsa." He laughed. "I haven't seen her for years. Why would she ask for me?"

"I have no idea. I only know that she did." Bernie slid up the wall slowly. So far, he held her gun loosely pointed in her direction. Keep it relaxed. Calm.

"I don't buy that." He stepped closer. "You came looking for me." He studied her. "You wanted to see the monster in person, maybe? The man who killed your sweet mamá? Maybe even arrest me."

His words struck too close to home, and she couldn't keep the truth from showing on her face.

"I knew it." He waved the gun at her. "That didn't go as planned, did it?"

"I admit." Bernie cast her eyes downward. "I came here with the thought of revenge. But when I arrived, my better instincts took over. Now, I just want to see you brought to justice."

"And how do you think you will do that?" He took another step toward her.

Bernie whipped out her baton and cracked him on the right wrist. The gun dropped and skittered across the floor. Isaac cursed and brought his left fist up, catching her in the chin. She flew backward onto the couch and managed to roll off before he could grab her. Now they faced each other.

"You were the little girl in the *bodega* all those years ago, weren't you?" Isaac's eyes gleamed in the semi-dark of the living room.

"Yes. Now I'm your worst nightmare." Hatred burned through her. *Dear God, help me control my anger.*

"But you're a cop. You can't kill me. You need to arrest me. Give me due process and all that ... stuff."

"I don't want to kill you. Haven't you been listening? Assaulting a policeman will do. I suggest you stop now and cut your losses."

His eyes darted to where her gun lay halfway between them.

"Don't try it, Isaac. It's time to surrender."

"And let you shoot me?"

"I told you I'm not interested in seeing you dead. At least not by my hand."

He bent his shaggy head and charged straight for Bernie. He grabbed for her, a hand closing on her jacket.

She slipped out, catching him behind the knee with her baton in one movement.

He fell, groaning and pressing her jacket against his injured knee.

She retrieved her gun, keeping aim on him. Sirens sounded and grew closer. She wiped sweat from her forehead. "Stay there. Don't move."

<hr />

DANIEL BACKED OFF THE ACCELERATOR. A group of Cincinnati police cars blocked the road outside the house they were headed for.

"Good. They're here." The tension in his chest eased.

"Pull as close as you can." Jeannie undid her seatbelt. As soon as the car stopped, she opened the door.

Daniel and Zoe ran to keep up with her. He spied Bernie's car in the middle of the mix. *Please, God, protect her.*

"Who's in charge here?" Jeannie flashed her ID and was directed to an officer with a bullhorn. Daniel and Zoe followed at a discreet distance. "I'm Detective Jeannie Jansen of the Pleasant Valley Police Department. My partner, Detective Santos, is in there."

"We got your call. A woman up the street saw Mr. West forcefully pull a woman inside earlier tonight, and she hasn't come out." The captain took off his hat and ran a hand across his bald head. "Another neighbor heard sounds of a struggle. What was she doing here?"

"I sent her ahead to let Mr. West know his niece has been hospitalized and wants to see him." Jeannie bit her lip. "When we couldn't raise her, we called you guys to investigate and came for support."

The captain peered at her. "This guy's a nasty one. I was just about to make initial contact." He offered the bullhorn to Jeannie.

She shook her head and pushed it away.

"Isaac West, this is the Cincinnati Police Department. We know you have Detective Santos inside. Why don't you and Detective Santos come outside with your hands where we can see them? We don't want anyone to get hurt."

The front door opened.

"Get ready." The captain spoke into his shoulder mic.

35

Daniel's heart twisted. He touched the cross against his chest. His eyes glued to the door, he moved forward through the crowd.

The door opened, and Bernie stepped onto the porch. "We're going to need an ambulance in—" She was yanked backward, out of sight.

Heart pounding, he sprinted across the lawn. Heavy footsteps sounded behind him with voices yelling for him to wait. He leaped onto the porch and kicked the door open. Big man. Straddling Bernie. His hands around her throat. Squeezing. Daniel roared and tackled the man, pushing him off the woman he loved. A red haze covered his vision. He cocked his arm, ready to hammer his fist into the man's body.

"Stop it!" Jeannie screamed as three officers grabbed his arms and pulled him off Isaac West. "That won't help things."

◄○▬▬▬▬▬▬▬▬▬▬▬○►

BERNIE SQUEEZED HER EYES SHUT. Every muscle in her body hurt. She groaned and turned on her side, pulling the covers over her head. Wait a minute. This wasn't her bed. Where was she?

She lifted one edge of the blanket and looked directly into the face of a character from Star Wars. She wasn't sure which one since she wasn't a fan. But she knew someone who was—Jeannie's son.

What was she doing in his bedroom? Curiosity overcame pain, and she sat up. She inspected the T-shirt and athletic shorts she had on. Were they his too? Time to find some answers. She padded into the kitchen. Jeannie leaned against the counter, arms crossed. Daniel sat at the table, hands wrapped around a mug.

"What's going on?"

Jeannie pulled a chair out for her. "Sit down." She brought over a steaming cup of coffee. "How are you feeling?"

"I feel like I've been in a ... fight." A frisson of fear ran through her. Had she done something wrong? Had she hurt someone?

A glance passed between the other two. "It must be the meds the doc gave her," Jeannie said to Daniel.

"You don't remember what happened last night?" Daniel said.

She shook her head.

"It's okay." He reached across the table. "It'll come back to you."

"Tell me." She drew back. "What did I do?" She gave each of them a piercing look. "I want to know."

Jeannie pulled out a chair. "You went after the man who killed your mother."

"But you didn't go through with it." His words tripped on Jeannie's.

"No." Jeannie shook her head. "He attacked you, tried to strangle you."

The memories rushed back. "I remember." She looked at Daniel. "You saved me."

"I was first through the door. The others were right behind me."

"Thank you. Both of you." She picked up her cup but sat it down again. "What happened to him?"

"Mr. West is in custody in Cincinnati. I'm going over later to interview him." Jeannie sat a plate of eggs and toast in front of Bernie. "That was smart the way you recorded everything on your phone. Now we have the evidence we need to convict him of your mother's murder."

"I need to go to the hospital and see my father." Bernie laid her napkin on the table and stood. "Is my car here?"

"It is, but I'll be glad to drive you," Daniel said.

She shook her head. "I need to get back to doing things for myself as soon as possible. I'll need to be at work tomorrow."

"Hang on." Jeannie raised a hand. "You took a pretty bad beating and were nearly strangled to death. You aren't going anywhere by yourself." She put a hand on her hip. "And as far as work, we'll see about that. Maybe paperwork, but—"

"If I want to see my father, I will see my father." Bernie's eyes narrowed. Dizziness overwhelmed her, and she eased back onto her chair.

Daniel glanced at Jeannie.

"On second thought," Bernie said. "Maybe I could use the help for now."

◁━━━━━━━━━━━━━▷

SOME OF THE bandages had been removed from her father.

"You're looking better." Bernie gave him a broad smile.

"They are feeding me good. Not as spicy as I like, but good."

She laughed. "When you get out of here, I'll fix you a real Mexican dinner." She stroked his cheek. "You rest and do everything the nurses say. Okay?"

"I will." He inspected her face. "But what happened to you, *mija*?"

"A little scuffle with a suspect." Her makeup must not have

been as good as she thought. "He lost." She smiled. "That's the job, Papá"

His eyes clouded. "I know, but I get worried."

"No need. I'm careful." But she wasn't, was she? She'd walked away from this one. What about the next time? There wouldn't be a next time. No more letting her emotions rule her head.

"I got him, Papá." She surveyed her father's bruised and beaten body. Her stomach roiled as she bent close to his ear. "I got the man who killed Mamá." She straightened and pushed her hand into her pocket. "I need to go now. See you later."

As she moved to leave, he grabbed her hand. "*Te amo, mija.*" A tear slipped from his eye and began its journey down his battered face.

"I love you too, Papá."

Daniel waited in the hall. "How is he?"

"Much better. Where's Jeannie?"

"She's talking to Elsa."

A surge of adrenaline shot through her. "Great. Let's go."

"Not so fast." Daniel put a hand on her arm. "Do you think that's such a good idea?"

"Why not?"

"She knows about her uncle."

"So?" What was he getting at?

"She blames you for him being in jail."

"That's ridiculous. He attacked me."

"I know, Bernie. But he's her family."

"All right. I'll look in on Ursula." She stabbed him with her gaze. "But I expect you to let me know everything that Elsa says to Jeannie."

"I will, but don't you think Jeannie will tell you herself?"

"Probably. Yes, of course. I'm ..."

"You're still not settled from the attack. And although you won't admit it, you're exhausted and need to rest. It takes a while. Go see Ursula, and we'll regroup later."

BERNIE PULLED up short as the door swung open to Ursula's room.

"This is a restricted area." A nurse faced her, then glanced at the policeman sitting by the door.

"I'm here to see your patient." Bernie displayed her credentials.

"She's unresponsive, but you're welcome to sit with her."

Bernie entered the cool semi-dark room. The only sound was the low hum of the monitor. She eased into the recliner next to the bed and studied Ursula Pidgeon. So pale. If it weren't for the rising and falling of her chest and the machines recording her vitals, she'd appear dead. Could she hear? Should Bernie speak to her?

She let her head relax against the chair cushion. It was nice to sit for a while. Peaceful. If she closed her eyes ...

Voices rose outside the door. She unsnapped her holster and crossed the room.

"Just ask Detective Santos. She knows me."

Zoe?

Bernie opened the door, bumping into the back of the guard.

"There she is. Ask her." Zoe gestured toward Bernie.

"It's okay. Sorry for the ruckus." Bernie motioned for her to be quiet. "Come in."

"I tried to save them, and I botched it." Zoe stopped inside the room, her violet eyes fixed on the woman lying so still before her. "If I'd gone into the farmhouse earlier, I could have gotten them out before the explosion."

"Or gotten yourself killed. Then who would have carried Elsa out?"

Zoe wiped a tear from her cheek. "I guess that's true."

Bernie's stomach growled. "Are you hungry?"

"I could get us some food."

"That would be great." Zoe needed a mission to keep her

happy, and Bernie looked forward to more recliner time. A twenty-minute nap would be nice.

Bernie woke up sixteen minutes later. She stood and stretched. Zoe should be back soon with the food. She stepped into the bathroom attached to Ursula's hospital room and pulled the door ajar. A glance in the mirror caused her to blink. Ouch. She looked like she'd been in a fight—wait a minute, she had been. She let out a soft chuckle.

No wonder her father noticed. She hadn't put on enough makeup to cover her black eyes and blotchy skin. She wet a paper towel and wiped her face.

A soft noise in the hospital room put her on alert. It was too soon for Zoe to be back, and she would have announced her return. Bernie willed her ears to detect the slightest sound.

"Mama?"

Every muscle in Bernie's body tensed. There was only one person who would call Ursula *Mama*. And he was dead.

Or was he?

36

B ernie waited. The extra chair in the room scraped across the floor. Was that sobbing? She nudged the bathroom door open with her foot and peeked into the room.

A man sat hunched over Ursula's bed, his back to her, his face buried in the crook of his arm lying next to her. His body shook with weeping.

Bernie moved slowly toward him. "Caleb?"

He sprang to his feet and faced her.

Half of his face looked normal. The other half suffered severe burns. She dug deep for the strength not to recoil at the sight of him. His hair was burnt completely away from melted skin, and his scalp was blackened and oozing.

"You need a doctor, Caleb." She motioned toward the phone. "Let me call one."

"No." He moved around the end of the bed toward the window. "There's no hope for me." He rolled up his left sleeve. "The whole side of my body is burned like this. What do I have to live for anyway?" His one good eye filled with tears. "I've messed everything up." He spun, yanked the blinds up, and opened the catch on the window.

"I can't let you do that." Bernie tackled him, rubbing flesh from his burned arm.

He cried out and landed a punch to her nose. "I deserve to die."

Pain filled her world. She pushed through the fog that threatened to engulf her. He'd gotten the window open and had a leg cocked to step through. She couldn't let that happen. She grabbed his belt with both hands and pulled hard.

Zoe pushed through the door holding two bags.

"I'm—" She dropped the food and raced to Bernie sitting on the floor with Caleb in her lap and a washcloth from the side table covering her nose.

"We need a doctor up here ASAP. And more police."

Caleb relaxed against her. She patted his good arm.

"Your mother's in a coma. But there's a good chance she'll recover. And Elsa's doing good. I'm sure both of those women would rather you lived. No matter what. That's the way love is."

"I wish I could believe that, Detective."

<hr />

THE NURSES' locker room proved to be a great place to get cleaned up. Bernie let the hot water run over her a few minutes longer. They even had a spare set of scrubs for her to wear. She gathered her things and stepped into the hallway.

"I can't leave you alone for a second." Jeannie rushed toward her. "I thought visiting a woman in a coma would be safe, but oh no. Not for you." She eyed Bernie's bandaged nose, and her face softened. "I should have known better. Glad you're okay. Good work. Caleb's been admitted, and we can talk to him."

Bernie steeled herself to see the disfigured body of Caleb again. But when she entered the room, his wounds had been dressed, and he lay comfortably under a clean white sheet. A sigh escaped her lips.

"That bad, huh?" He fixed his one good eye on her.

"You look much better." She shook her head. "How do you feel?"

"Okay, I guess. The doc gave me lots of good meds."

"Caleb, we know most everything about what happened to your dad, but there are a few details we need to clear up." Jeannie scooted a chair next to the bed. "And, it seems you may be able to help us with that."

He cleared his throat. "Can I have a drink of water?"

Bernie offered him the cup with a straw.

"I'm recording our conversation on my phone. Is that okay?" He agreed

"When you were in the house with Amber, what did she say?" She held her phone close to him.

He closed his uninjured eye. Had he fallen asleep?

"She blamed them for her son's death. All of them. Dad, Mom, Belkin—"

"But not Abbott. She didn't know about Abbott, did she?"

He shook his head.

"Amber told us she saw your truck outside Abbott's house the day he was murdered." Jeannie paused. "Did you kill Henry Abbott, Caleb?"

Caleb sank into his bed, his eye closed.

"I think it's time we let him rest." Bernie caught Jeannie's attention. "We can come back later."

Outside his room, Jeannie rounded on Bernie. "Why did you interfere with my questioning?"

"Because any lawyer worth his degree would get it thrown out as badgering a witness. He's in a hospital bed recovering from burns and heavily medicated."

"You're right." Jeannie pressed her lips together. "I hate having to stop an interview, and I hate lawyers."

"I know." Bernie sighed. All she wanted was a cold drink, two aspirins, and bed. "Let's go see if Elsa's story matches Caleb's."

"Good idea."

At Elsa's room, Jeannie knocked and entered. Elsa sat in a recliner by the windows, speaking to someone on her cell phone.

"I have to go now. Remember what I said." She pressed *End* and laid her phone on her lap. "Detectives. Have you found Caleb's body?"

"We have good news. He's alive." Jeannie stepped closer.

"Where is he?" Elsa rose. Her phone slid to the floor. "Can I see him?"

Bernie retrieved the phone and pressed the screen, but it was locked. She handed it to Elsa.

"He's here. He's being treated for third-degree burns and can't have any visitors yet. I'll let you know when that changes." Jeannie removed her phone from her pocket. "We're here to ask a few questions."

"I'll do the best I can."

"When Mrs. Nayar held you hostage, did she tell you why?"

"She wanted to avenge her son's death."

"Did she blame all of you?"

Elsa swiped a hand across her forehead. "She said she blamed Ursula, Ms. Belkin, and Dean Major. Caleb got caught up in it because he's Ursula's brother, and—"

"What about your brother Henry Abbott?" Jeannie said.

"Yes. Him too," Elsa said. "Oh dear, do you think she killed my brother?"

"No, all the evidence points to Caleb, and he as much as told us he did it," Bernie said.

Elsa turned toward the window.

"But I don't think he killed your brother. I think it was you."

"That's not true." She spat the words into the air like a cobra spitting venom.

"I think it might be. Either you killed Abbott or Caleb did acting on your behalf. But my money's on you. I think you borrowed Caleb's truck. Drove over to your brother's house. And killed him. And I think Caleb knows it was you but loves you so much that he's willing to take the blame."

Bernie stared at the woman in the recliner. "The question becomes, how much do you love him? Are you willing to let him go to prison for the rest of his life for a crime he didn't commit?"

37

"You're right, Detective." Elsa's head dropped to her chest. "I killed my brother." Elsa raised her face. "He was a hateful man who hurt so many people. I didn't want anyone else I loved to suffer."

Jeannie read Elsa her rights. She arranged for a woman officer to be with her along with another policeman stationed outside her door.

As Bernie pushed through the hospital doors, she probed the bandages on her nose. "I could really use something to eat and some rest."

"Soon." Jeannie climbed into the driver's seat of their car. "We have one more mystery to solve. Who shot at Daniel? And blew up his car?"

"Since Ursula and Caleb kidnapped his aunt, I'm pretty sure they did the rest. But you're right. There may be more to it. We need to speak to Daniel again." She could feel Jeannie's eyes on her. "What?"

"How did you know it wasn't Caleb who killed Henry Abbott?"

"Caleb's not a killer." Bernie shook her head. "Assuming he's the one who shot at Daniel, he deliberately missed every time."

"Sure." Jeannie sneered. "He just makes bombs for a living."

"But that's not the same as killing someone up close and personal. And when he could have shot you in Elsa's yard, he knocked you down instead." She clicked her seatbelt into place. "But Elsa was a woman with a grudge. I'll phone Daniel when we get back to the station." She reclined her seat and closed her eyes.

⊶——————————⊷

NO NEED TO CALL DANIEL. He and Zoe stood by Bernie's desk when they arrived.

"Good. Just the two people we're looking for," Jeannie said. "We need statements from both of you. Doc, you first." Jeannie keyed her computer to life. "We need to clear up a few details— like who shot at you, bombed your car, and why." She raised one eyebrow at him. "Got any suggestions?"

"This might help." Daniel took an envelope from his coat pocket and slid it across the desk. "It's information on a homegrown terrorist cell that's working in the area." He tapped the paper, glanced at Bernie and frowned. "You should be resting."

"Later, Daniel," she said. "We need to wrap this up."

"Caleb was a bomb maker for hire. He worked for this group and others. The second explosion at Elsa's farm? The one involving the barn? That was where Caleb made his bombs. I believe they thought I was sent here to assassinate Ghazzi. After he died, Caleb and others were afraid I was sizing their cell up for a take-over. They wanted me gone."

"Why call attention to themselves?" Jeannie said. "If they'd let it alone, you would have left anyway."

Daniel snapped his attention back to Jeannie. "No. After Ghazzi was murdered, my bosses tasked me with finding his killer. I wasn't going anywhere."

"So, they thought they could scare you away?"

"I suppose so. They weren't stupid. Look how long they managed to operate in Pleasant Valley without anyone noticing." He bit his lip. "And when they kidnapped Aunt Rose, they almost succeeded in convincing me to leave."

Jeannie swiveled to face her computer. "But in the end, the good guys win again."

"Which reminds me." Daniel turned to Bernie. "Remember when I told you about Ghazzi faking his death? And how some important papers went missing?"

She exchanged a look with Jeannie. "Do you think they could be the documents we received from Abbott's lawyer?"

"Could be." Jeannie rifled through her desk and withdrew the manila envelope. She passed it to Daniel along with a pair of gloves.

As he read, the corners of his mouth turned up in a satisfied smile. "These are the papers we've been looking for." His smile disappeared, replaced by a stony look. "Did you read them?"

"We read enough to know they were well over our paygrade." Daniel's face relaxed.

"Abbott's lawyer brought them to us per instructions from his will." Jeannie placed a form in front of him. "Sign here, and they're yours."

"Huh. So, we were wrong. Ghazzi never had them. Abbott did." Daniel shook his head. "Is there anything else you need from me? If not, I need to call my boss."

"I can't think of anything." Jeannie glanced around. "Zoe, you're next."

The private investigator took a seat between Bernie and Jeannie.

"How's your nose?" Zoe's voice filled with concern.

"It only hurts when I breathe." Bernie smiled. "We need you to write down what happened this afternoon in your own words." She pushed a pad toward the woman.

"Sure." She chose a pen from the Cardinals coffee cup on Jeannie's desk. "Daniel was worried about you."

Her pulse quickened. "You told him?"

"He asked how you were." Zoe frowned.

Bernie massaged her temples.

"Are you all right?" Zoe said.

"I need another aspirin." Bernie gave in to the pain. "I'll be back in a minute." She grabbed her purse and headed for the bathroom. What was going on? She never got sick. Nausea rolled over her in waves.

<hr />

BERNIE OPENED HER EYES. Daniel gazed down at her. She raised her hand.

"Lie still." He gave her a gentle smile and replaced her arm at her side. "You have a mild concussion."

"From a broken nose?"

"No. From hitting your head after you were punched. There's a good size lump there."

Pain arrowed through her skull. She gulped. "What now?"

"I suggest bedrest, drink water, and take something for the pain. I can prescribe something stronger than over the counter." He helped her sit up. "Do you have somewhere to stay?"

She nodded, but the movement caused her to moan. "My house is finished."

"Good. Zoe offered to stay with you for a day or so until you feel better." He raised his arms. "Don't argue. It's either that or the hospital."

"Where will you be?"

"Don't worry." His voice dropped to a whisper. "I'll be close."

<hr />

A WHISTLE DREW Bernie's attention away from her book.

"Hi, Handsome." Lori squawked from her perch near the front window.

"Who do you see, girl?" Bernie rose from the couch.

Lori began to preen her already splendid feathers.

"Must be Daniel." Bernie grinned and walked over to check. Yep. She opened the door before he could knock.

"How'd you know it was me? You could have been opening the door on a robber."

"Your girlfriend spotted your car." Bernie pointed to Lori.

He turned and raised his hand. Lori landed on his forearm.

"That means she wants to snuggle against your chest. Cross your arms. She's still a little unsettled and in need of comfort."

He did as he was told, and the parrot moved close to him, laying her head against his body.

"I think she likes to hear the heartbeat." Bernie led the way to her sofa. "Like a baby. It's soothing."

"I'm glad she's back with you where she belongs." He stroked the bird's back. "You're good for each other."

"I do love her ... I just feel bad that she's here alone so much. Parrots need lots of interaction."

"Maybe you should get her a friend?"

Bernie frowned at him. "Two parrots? I don't know if my budget or my patience will stretch that far, but I'll think about it."

"Or your dad could come live with you, and she wouldn't be alone?"

"Oh, no." Bernie shook her head. "I like my privacy too much."

"How is your dad? Have you talked with him lately?"

"He's doing well. Out of the hospital and visiting my brother, Ricardo, in Chicago for a while." She twirled the ring on her right hand. "Rickie owns a grocery store up there, and he'll be sure Papá has plenty to do. It'll be good for him."

"I've noticed you playing with that ring before. Is it special to you?" He touched her hand.

"It was my mother's." Her eyes grew moist. "After all these years...I can't believe I..."

"I know." He put an arm around her and drew her close.

She leaned against him. Maybe Lori wasn't the only one who still needed comforting.

38

Bernie pulled into her parking space at the police station. The leaves on the oaks and maples were a brilliant mixture of reds, yellows, and greens. Four days off had seemed like a year. Zoe had to return to work after a couple of days, and if it hadn't been for Daniel visiting in the evenings, she might have gone mad.

She pushed through the doors to the precinct and slowed. Jeannie squinted at her computer screen.

Bernie walked over and picked up her glasses. "Here."

"Santos. Glad to see you back." A smile lit her partner's face.

"Glad to be back. What did I miss?"

"Nothing much." Jeannie pushed her chair away from her desk. "I sent an officer to interview Mrs. Nayar's neighbor and discovered she owns a white sedan. Guess who borrowed it occasionally?"

"Amber Nayar."

"And do you remember that strange box we found in her bedroom? It's for a wig. A red wig, to be exact. We found it and the long, hooded coat partially burned at the back of her property."

"You've been busy." Bernie grinned. "Anything else I should know?"

"Only that Elsa pled guilty to murdering her brother. Ursula woke from her coma and collaborated Caleb's and Elsa's story about Amber Nayar.

"Caleb admitted he shot at Daniel, and that other members of the cell bombed Daniel's car and threatened him. And the FBI should have the terrorists rounded up by the end of the week."

"I still can't believe we had a terrorist cell here in Pleasant Valley." Bernie eased into her chair.

"Apparently, it's been active for a long time. If Amber Nayar hadn't been driven to get revenge for her son, we may never have discovered it."

"And if Daniel hadn't been here looking for Ghazzi, we might never have realized who Major was."

"Lots of ifs in this one."

"Yes." Bernie stuck her hand in her pocket. One other big one could end up breaking her heart. "Have you seen Daniel today?"

"Right here, darlin'" His deep voice sounded from behind her.

She startled.

"I need your help with something." He looked at Jeannie. "May I borrow your partner for a moment?"

"Be my guest." Jeannie grinned.

He took Bernie by the hand and led her outside away from the parked cars. Picnic tables stood under the oak trees by the precinct for the use of those who worked in the building.

"Let's sit."

What was he up to? Bernie chose a bench.

He sat next to her and took her hand. "Now that my work is done, I should be heading back to Cleveland. What do you think?"

What was he asking her? She probed his blue eyes and scanned his handsome face for signs. Surely, she could figure this out. Did he want permission to go? Or did he want her to ask him to stay?

And what did she want? He said he'd come clean about everything, but had he? Could she trust him? She could love this man. She *did* love this man.

A lump formed in her throat. "Is there someone special in Cleveland?"

"No." He stroked her fingers.

"I don't know what to say. I love you, but I'm so frightened." The words burst from her throat, unbidden.

"Then that settles it." He smiled at her. "Because I love you too. And I'm scared to death." He kissed the back of her hand. "We'll take it one day at a time, my sweet Bernie. One beautiful day at a time." He leaned in to gather her in his arms.

"Ouch." Her nose.

Laughing, he picked her up and placed her on the tabletop. Leaning down, he brought his mouth to hers for a soft kiss that grew more intense as the moments passed.

And she knew she'd read the clues correctly.

◁——————————▷

"I'm TOLD I have you to thank for my favorite nephew sticking around." Rose O'Leary bustled over to Bernie's desk in her usual manner.

"He's decided to transfer to the office down here. I'm not sure how much I had to do with it." Bernie grinned at her.

"Girl, you're glowing." Rose kissed her on the cheek. "Thank you."

"We're back." The doors to the precinct opened, and the voices of Captain Nate Zuberi and Madison Long Zuberi blended in, announcing their return.

Jeannie and Bernie greeted them.

"So, what have we missed?" Nate eyed the bandages on Jeannie's arm and Bernie's nose.

The two detectives looked at each other.

"Not much. Been pretty quiet here, boss."

ABOUT THE AUTHOR

Deborah Sprinkle is a retired chemistry teacher among other things. So it should come as no surprise that the protagonist in her debut novel, "Deadly Guardian", is one as well. Mrs. Sprinkle is also co-author of a non-fiction book entitled "Exploring the Faith of America's Presidents". She has won awards for her short stories, articles, and her latest novel, "Death of an Imposter". Mrs. Sprinkle lives in Memphis with her husband where she continues to be an ordinary woman serving an extraordinary God.

Deadly Guardian

Trouble in Pleasant Valley - Book One

When the men she dated begin dying, Madison Long must convince the police of her innocence and help them determine who has taken on the role of her guardian before he kills the only man she ever truly loved, Detective Nate Zuberi.

Madison Long, a high school chemistry teacher, looks forward to a relaxing summer break. Instead, she suffers through a nightmare of threats, terror, and death. When she finds a man murdered she once dated, Detective Nate Zuberi is assigned to the case, and in the midst of chaos, attraction blossoms into love.

Together, she and Nate search for her deadly guardian before he decides the only way to truly save her from what he considers a hurtful relationship is to kill her—and her policeman boyfriend as well.

MORE ROMANTIC SUSPENSE FROM SCRIVENINGS PRESS

Hostage

Her confidence shot, Agent Macy Packer desperately wants to go back to her regular life, before she was taken hostage. To forget the pain, the fear and forget the man that helped her through all of it, then disappeared.

Kane Bledsoe is finally healed, his scars serving as a reminder of his time in captivity. But all he can think about is the blue-eyed woman that saved him. She had saved them all and left him with a burning hope.

A chance meeting and an attack prove Macy is still in danger. Kane pushes himself into the investigation, doing what he can to provide protection.

The enemy is clear, he wants Macy.

Kane will have to decide just how far he's willing to go to protect her. Can he sacrifice himself when the time comes?

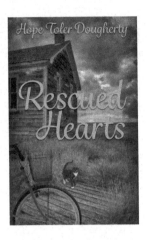

Rescued Hearts

Mary Wade Kimball's soft spot for animals leads to a hostage situation when she spots a briar-entangled kitten in front of an abandoned house. Beaten, bound, and gagged, Mary Wade loses hope for escape.

Discovering the kidnapped woman ratchets the complications for undercover agent Brett Davis. Weighing the difference of ruining his three months' investigation against the woman's safety, Brett forsakes his mission and helps her escape the bent-on-revenge brutes following behind. When Mary Wade's safety is threatened once more, Brett rescues her again. This time, her personal safety isn't the only thing in jeopardy. Her heart is endangered as well.

Song in the Dark

On the other side of darkness lies freedom ...

Hades/Persephone Inspired Romantic Suspense

After graduating from Juilliard, harpist Jenna Fields returns home to Albany to escape her manipulative ex. But coming home means dealing with her mother who has orchestrated every detail of Jenna's life. Waiting for a job offer that will allow her to escape New York and build a life of her own, Jenna volunteers to raise money for a local charity.

Homicide detective Dean Blackburn spends his days seeking justice for the dead. But death taints everything including him. When his three Dobermans lead him to Jenna, he tries to resist the little siren. She not only starts a fire in his heart but brings light and joy to his lonely world.

When her world crumbles beneath her feet and her dark secret revealed, Dean helps Jenna see that the key to escaping her mother's gilded cage is already in her hands.

Scrivenings
PRESS
Quench your thirst for story.
www.ScriveningsPress.com

Stay up-to-date on your favorite books and authors with our free e-newsletters.

ScriveningsPress.com